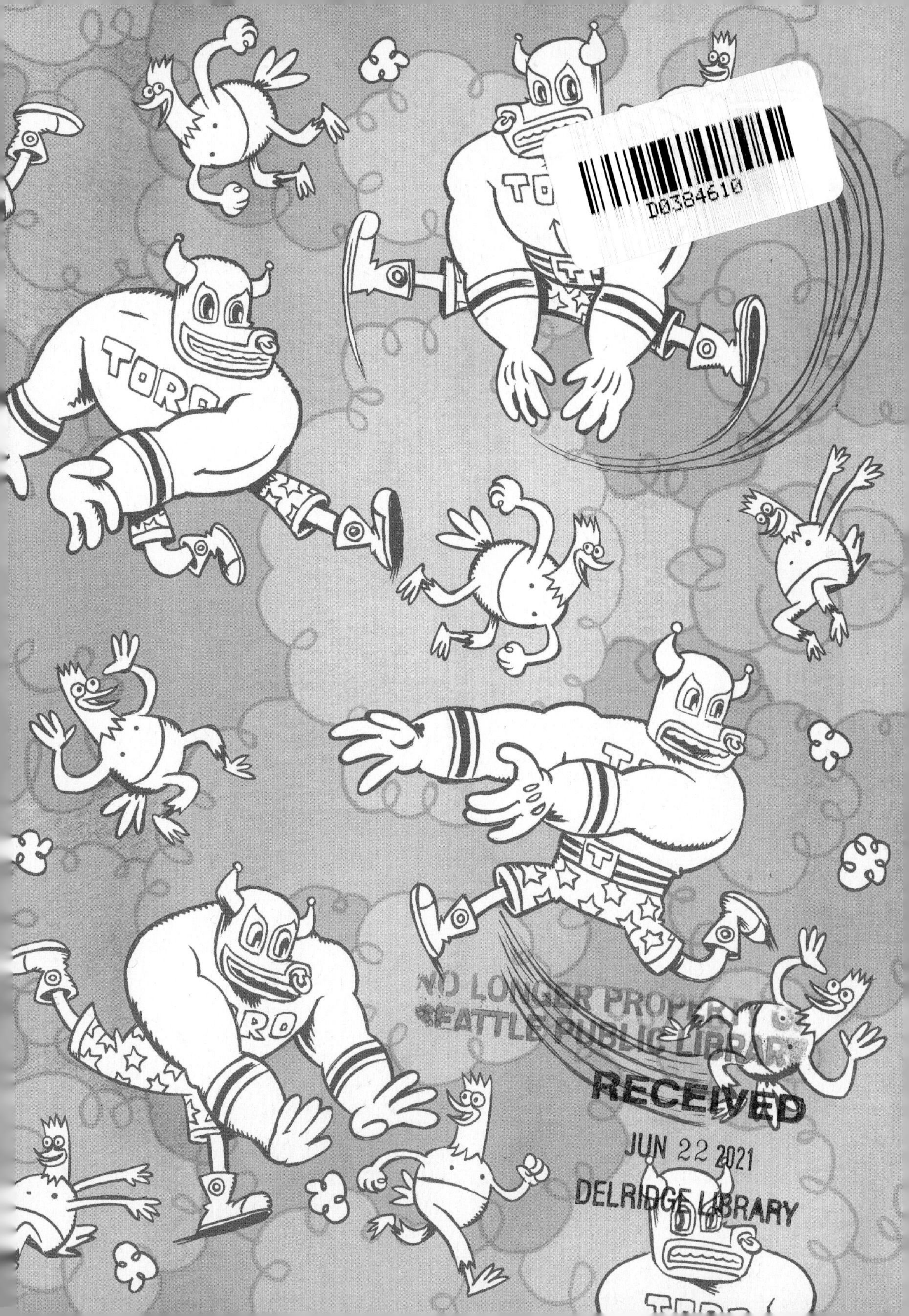

El Toro & Friends

Training Day

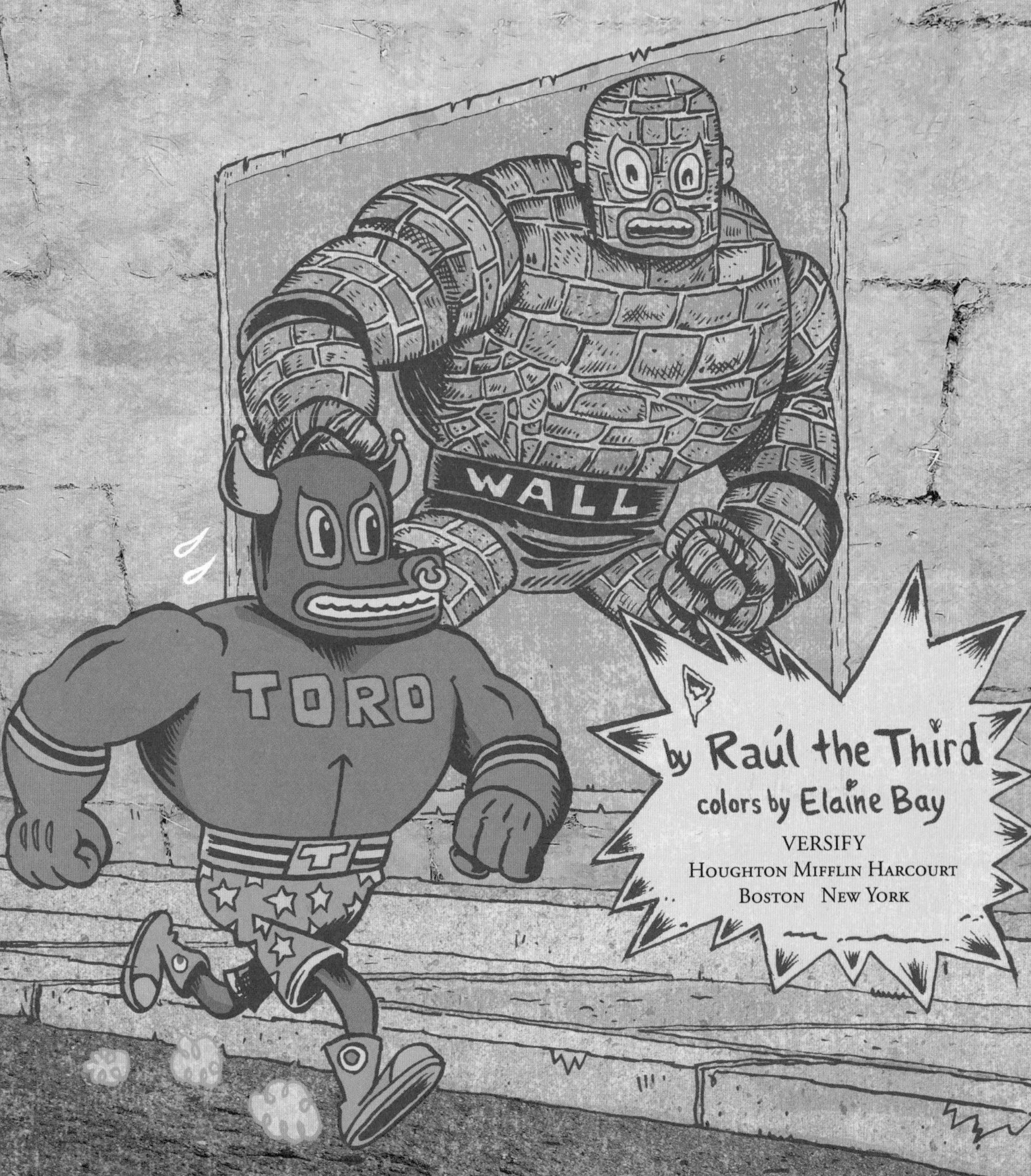
WALL
TORO

by Raúl the Third
colors by Elaine Bay

VERSIFY
Houghton Mifflin Harcourt
Boston New York

El Toro has a big match soon!
He wants to be Champion of the
World! ¡El Campeón del Mundo!

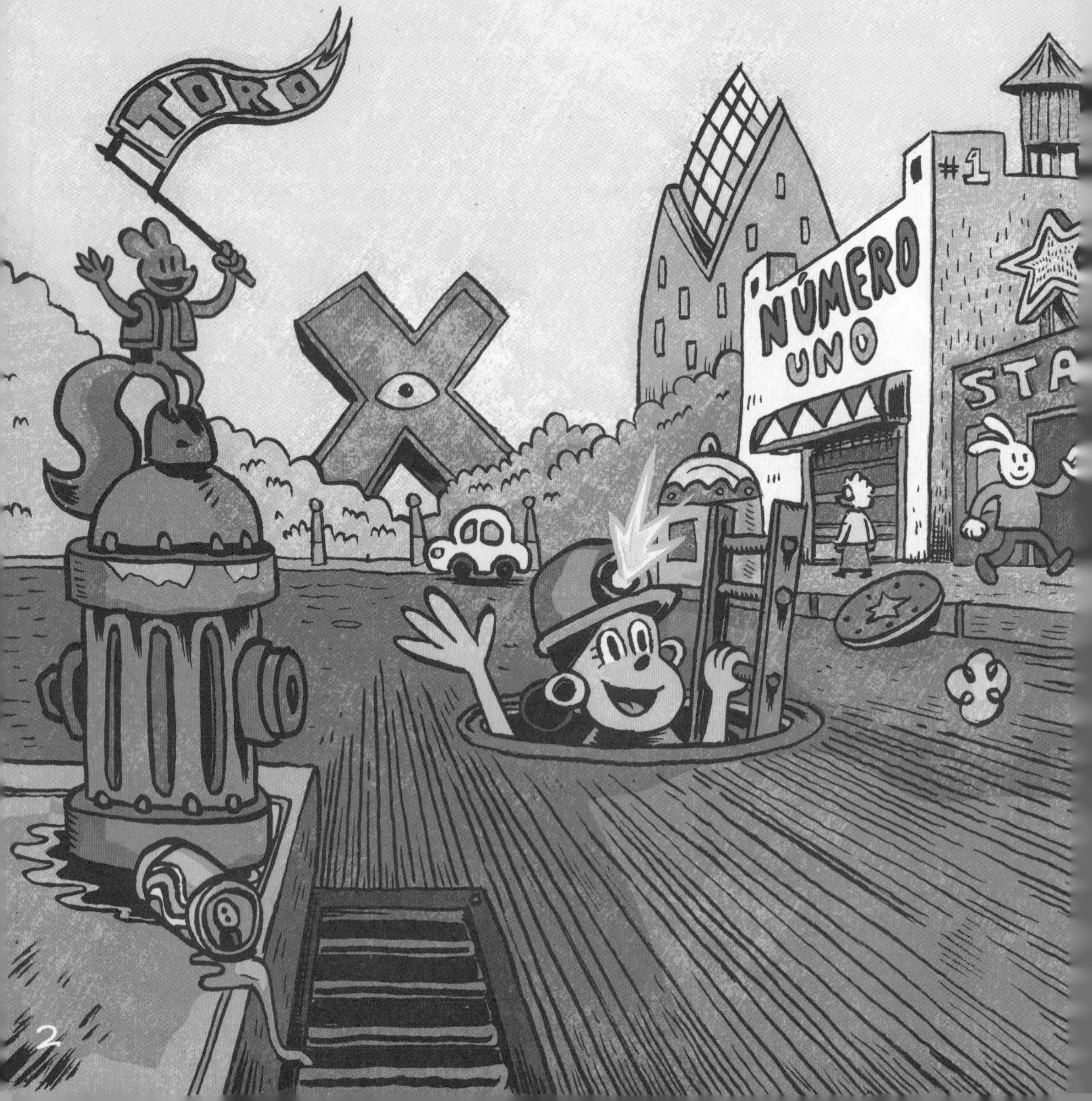
TORO
NÚMERO
UNO
#1

Number one! ¡Número uno!

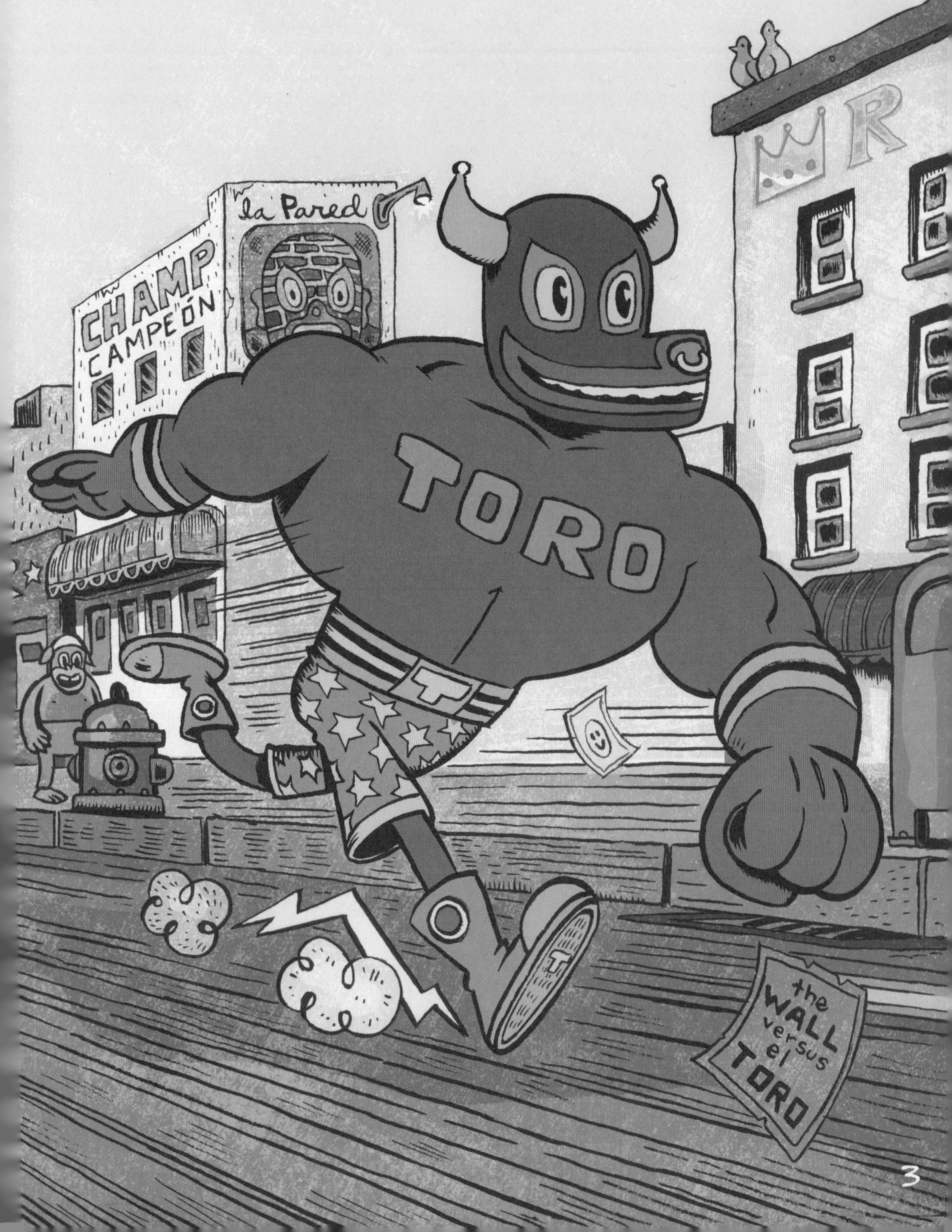
la Pared
CHAMP
CAMPEÓN
R
TORO
the WALL versus el TORO

El Toro has battled his way to the top. Match after match.

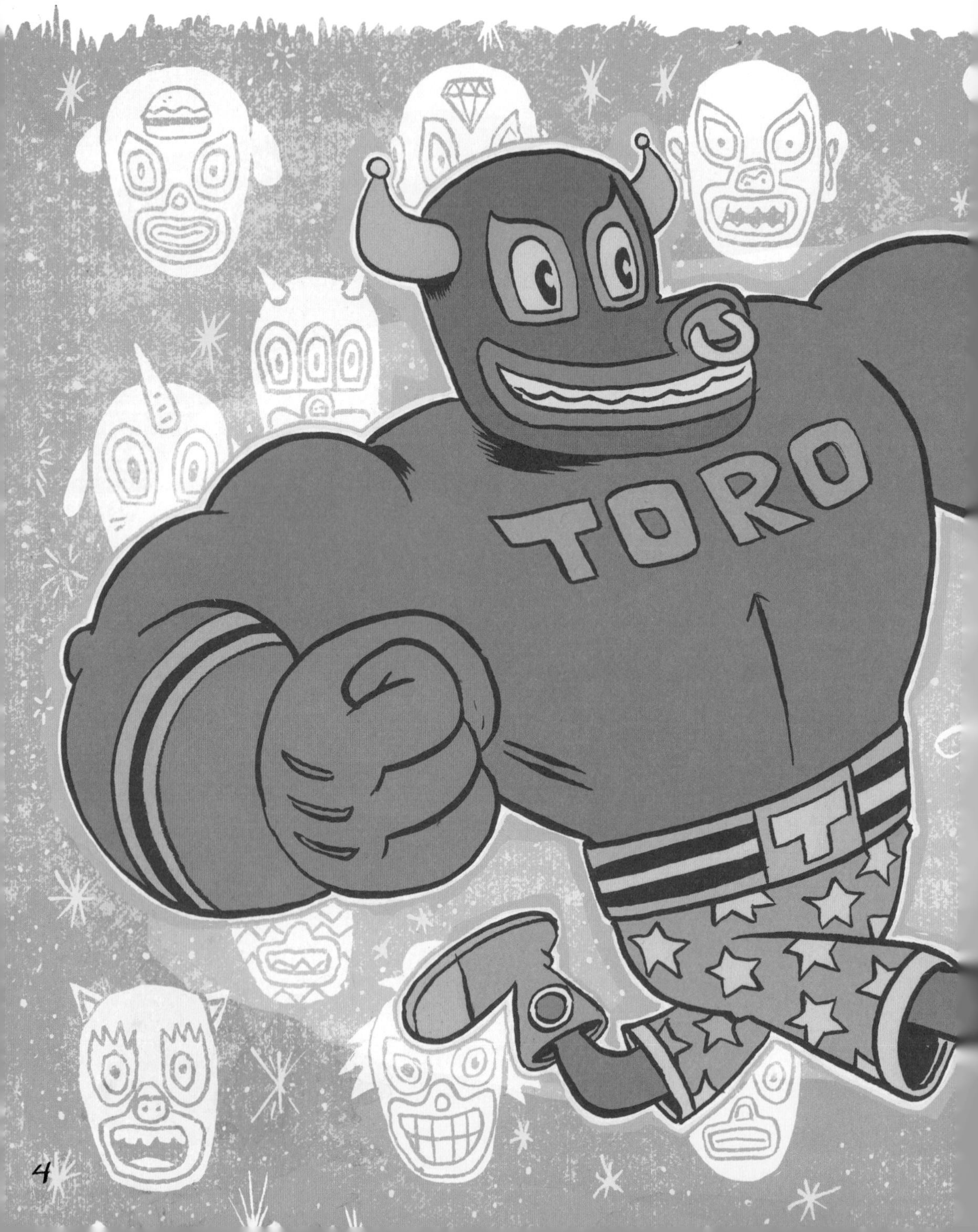
TORO
T

Now he will wrestle The Wall! The Wall is the undefeated champion of the world.

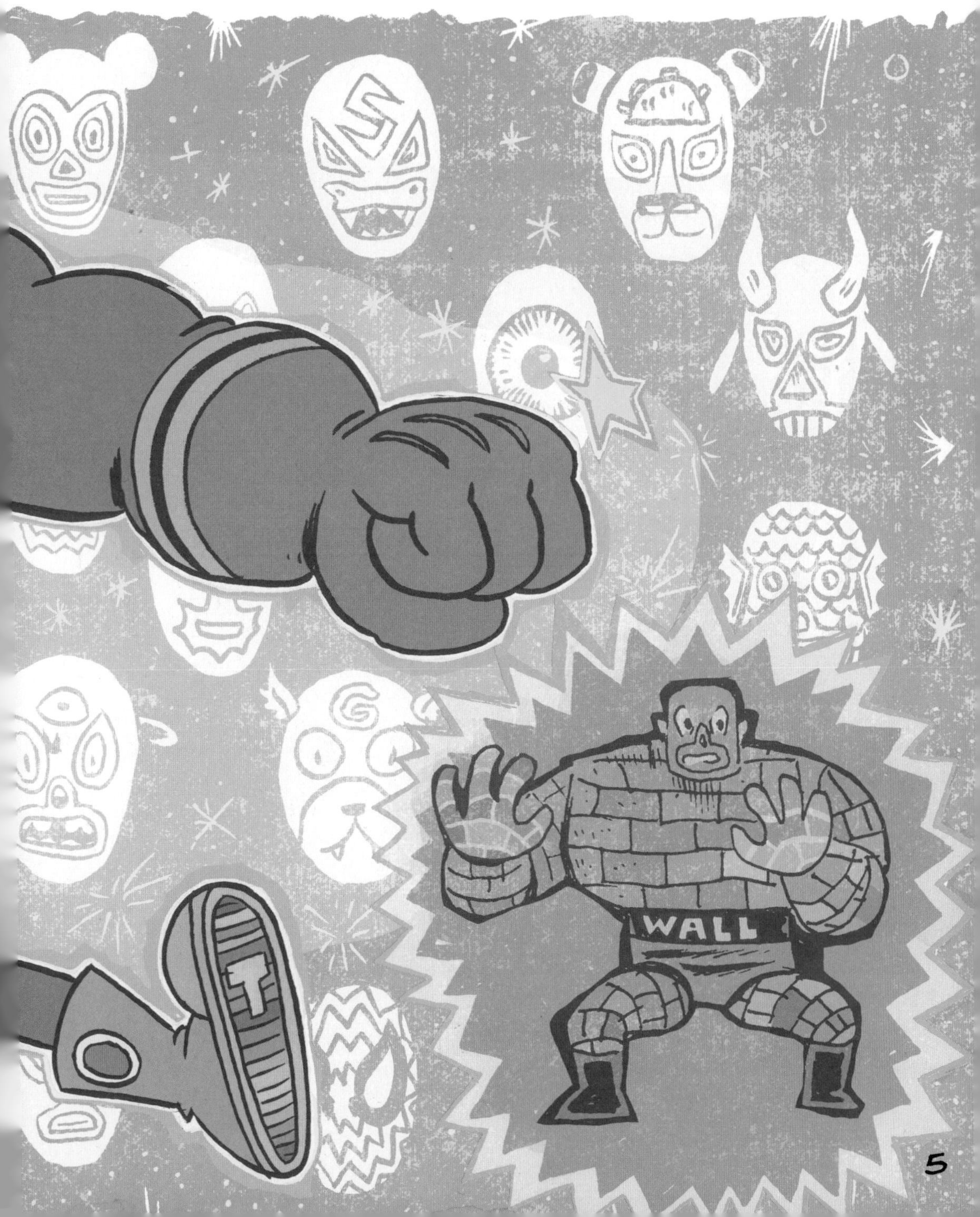
WALL

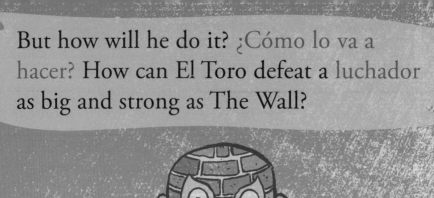

But how will he do it? ¿Cómo lo va a hacer? How can El Toro defeat a luchador as big and strong as The Wall?

Meet his trainer, Kooky Dooky.

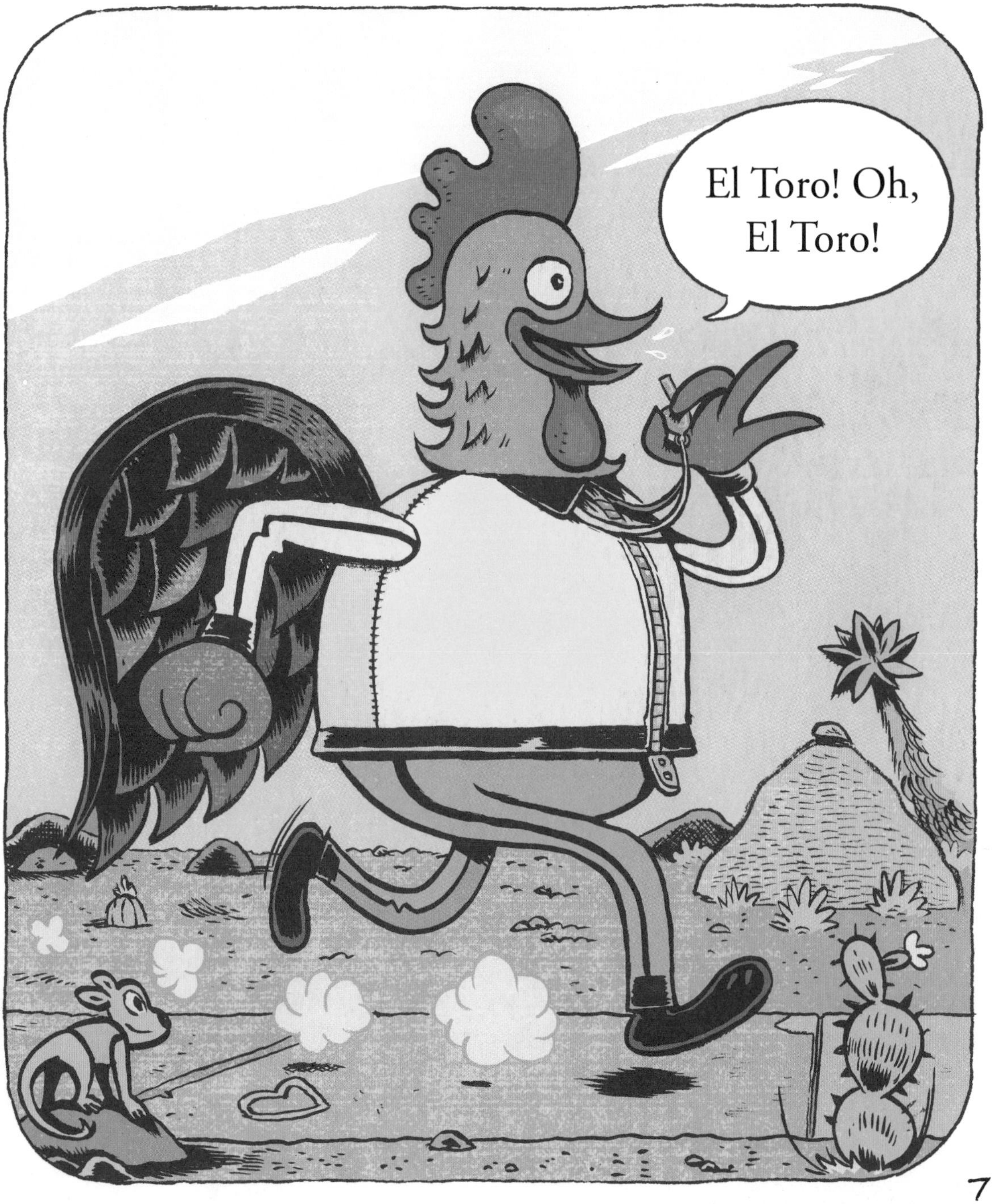
El Toro! Oh, El Toro!

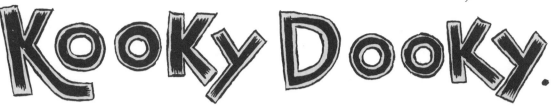

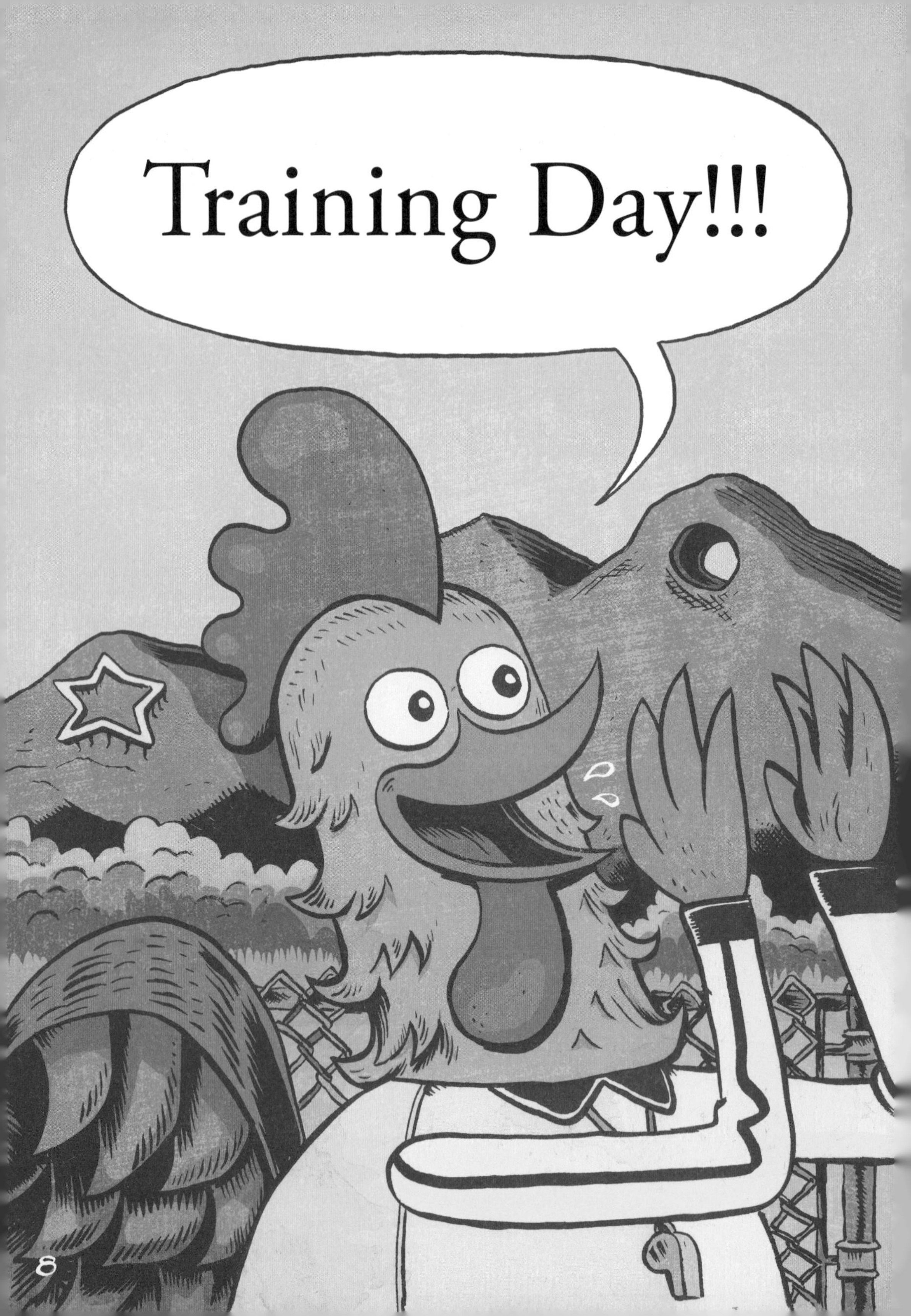
Training Day!!!

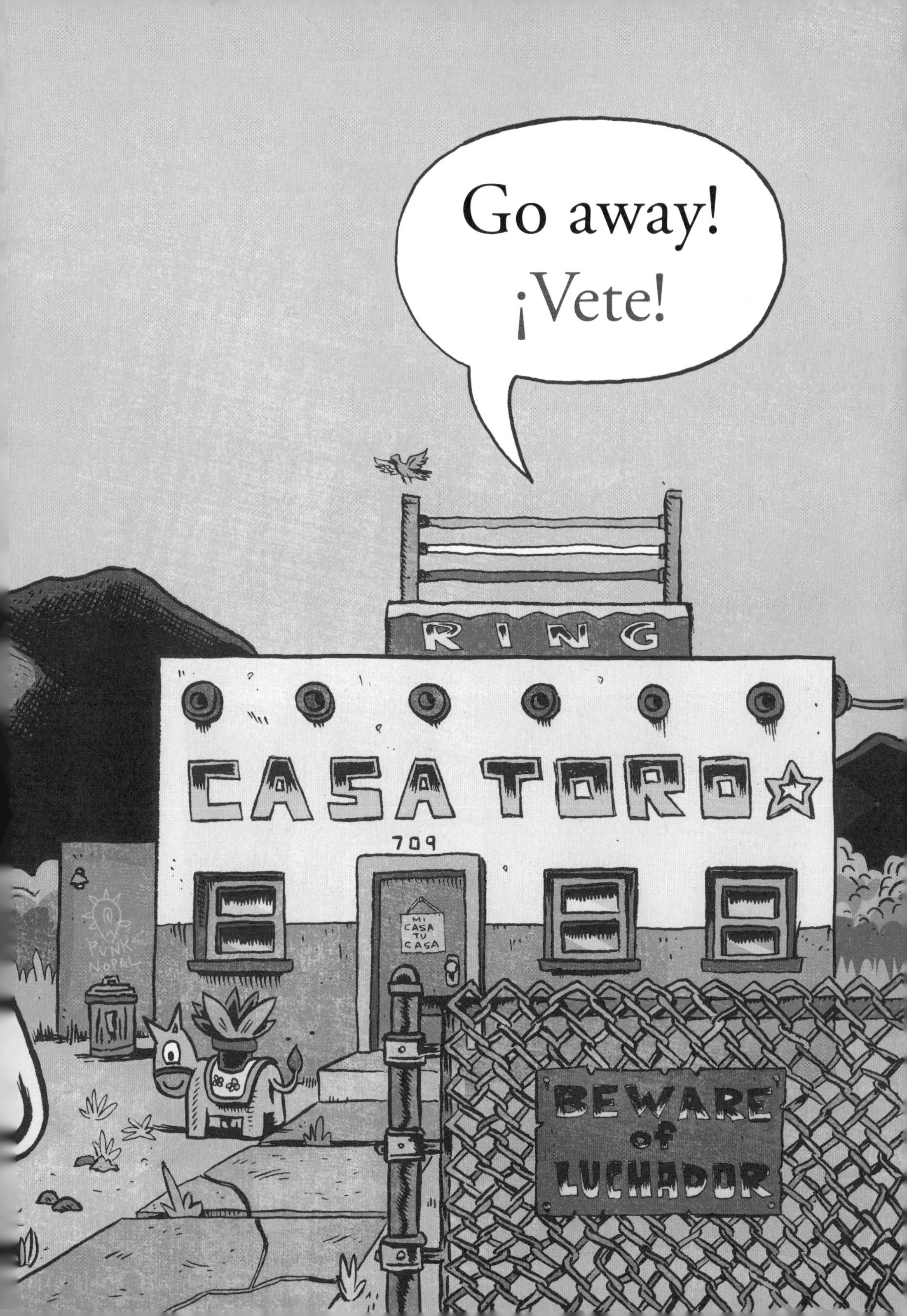
Go away!
¡Vete!
RING
CASA TORO
709
MI CASA TU CASA
PUNK NOPAL
BEWARE of LUCHADOR

El Toro does not feel like training today.

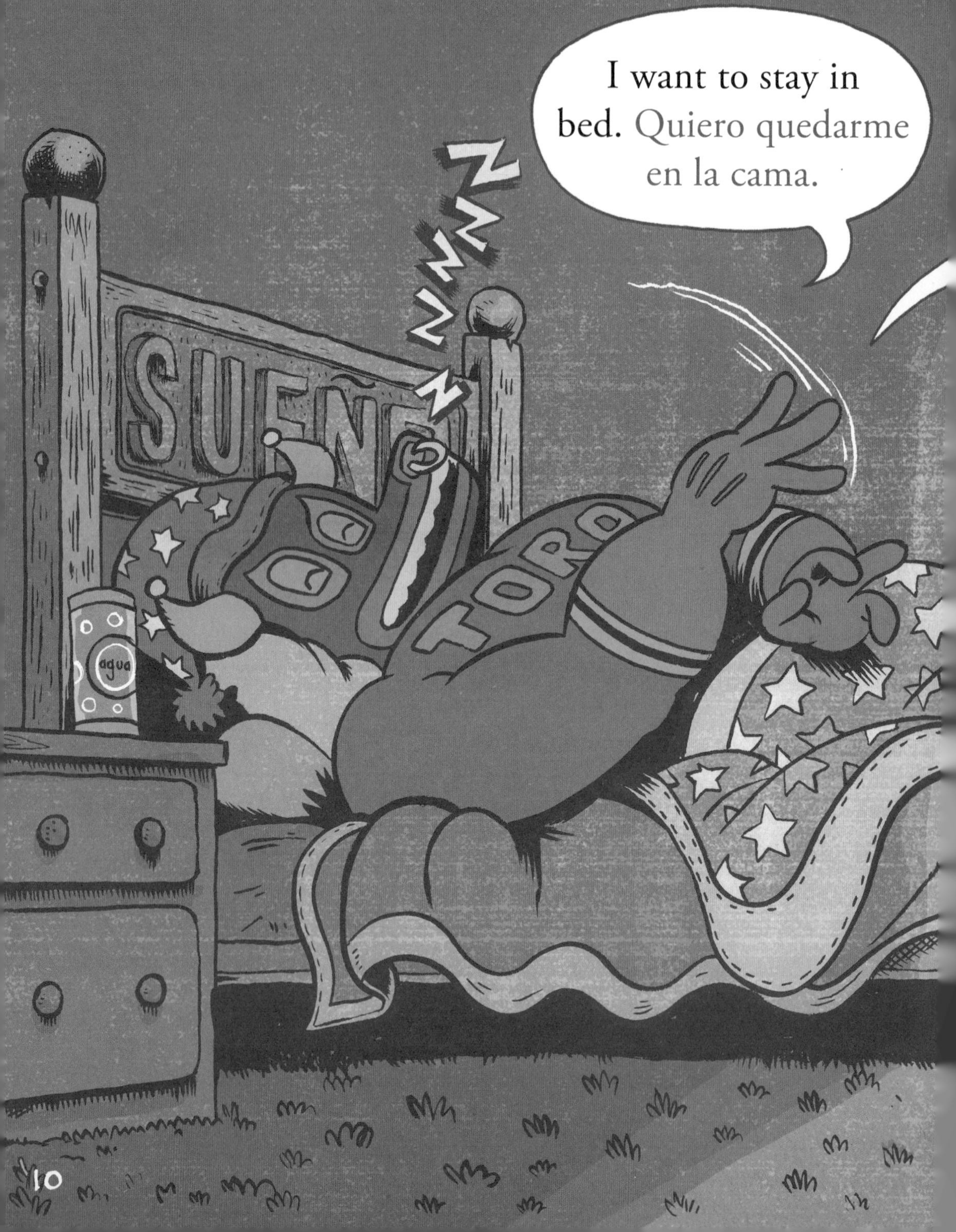
I want to stay in bed. Quiero quedarme en la cama.
agua
TORO

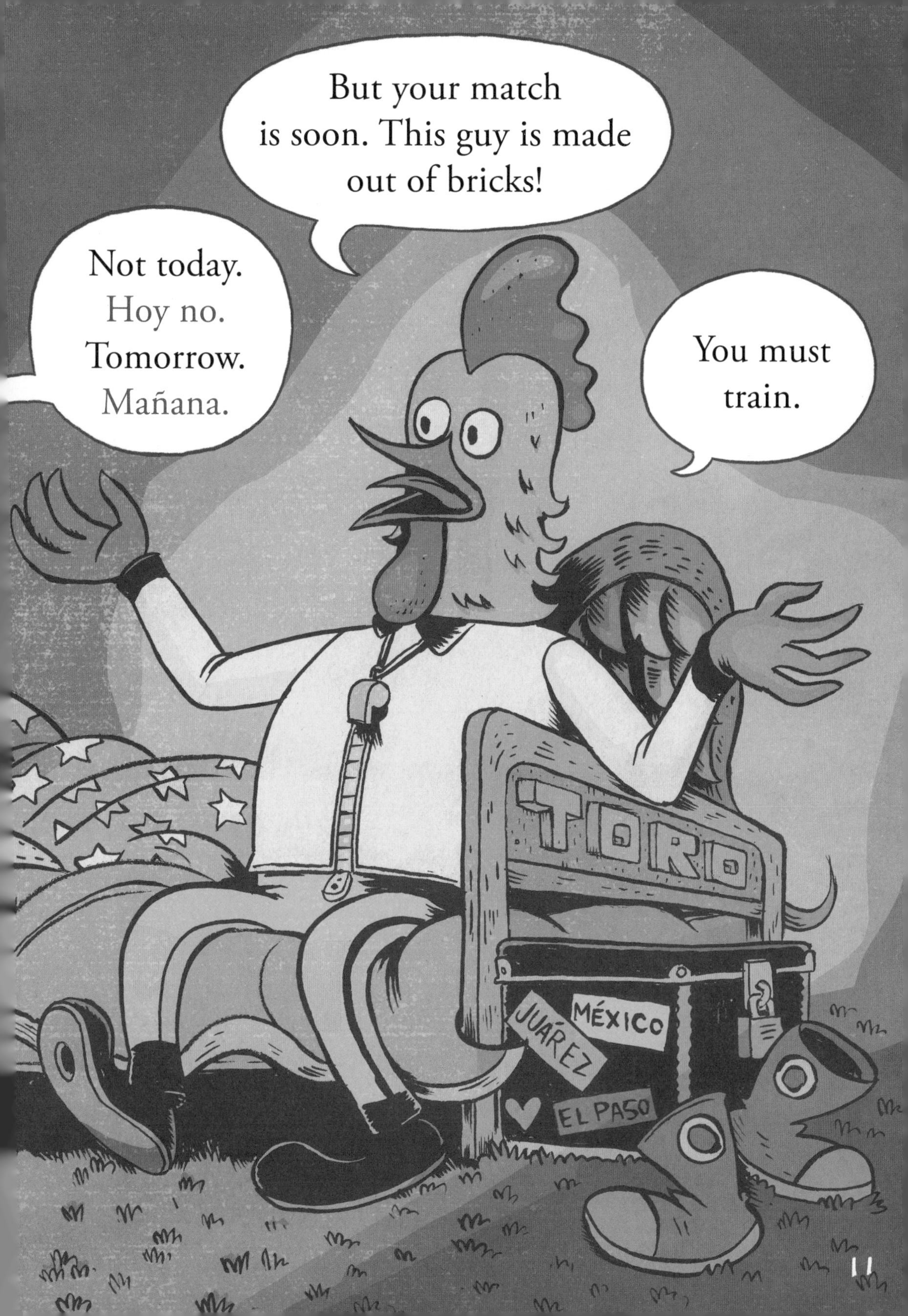

But your match is soon. This guy is made out of bricks!
Not today. Hoy no. Tomorrow. Mañana.
You must train.
TORO
JUÁREZ
MÉXICO
EL PASO

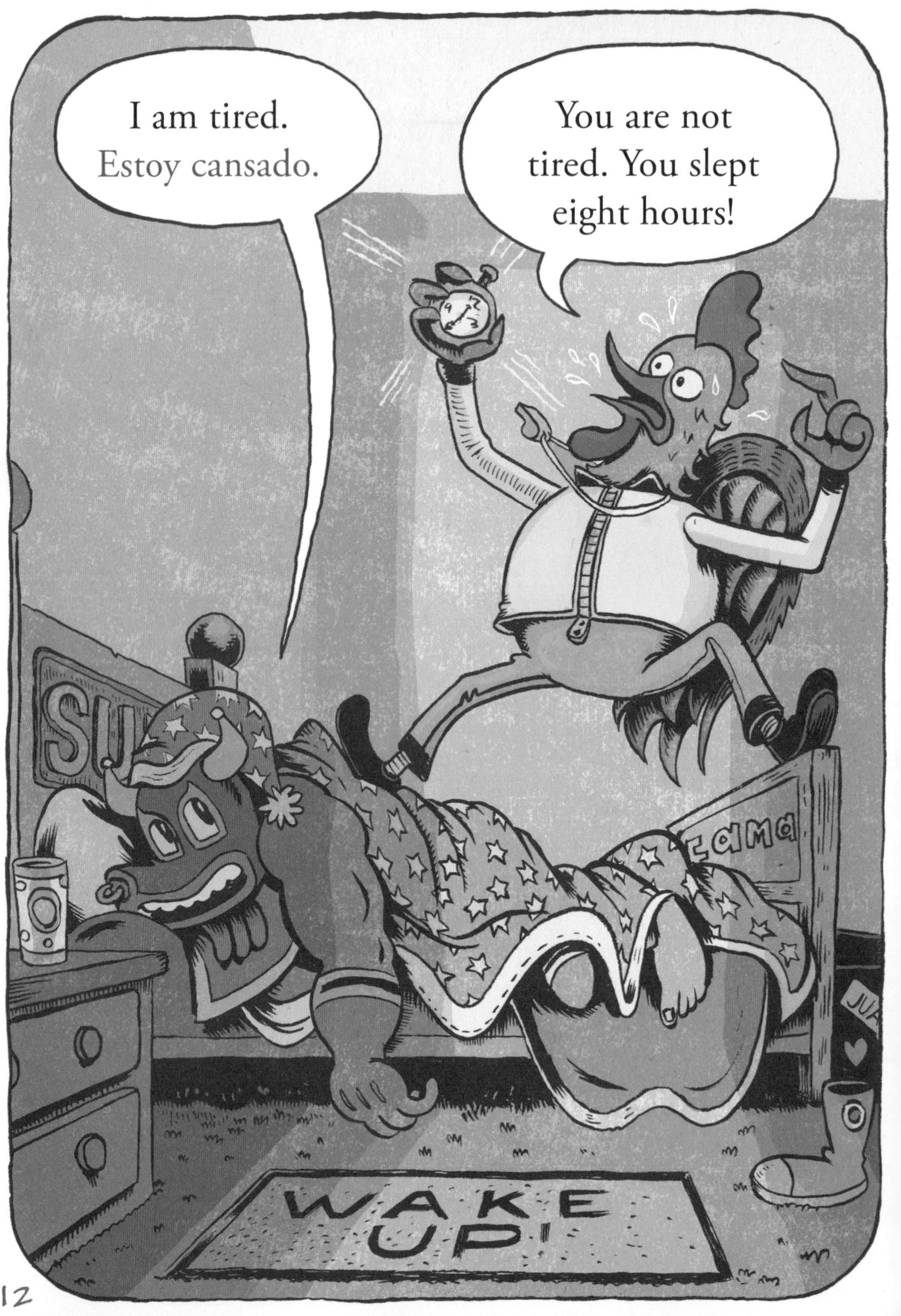
I am tired.
Estoy cansado.
You are not tired. You slept eight hours!
cama
WAKE UP!

Kooky Dooky has an idea! He will make breakfast for El Toro.

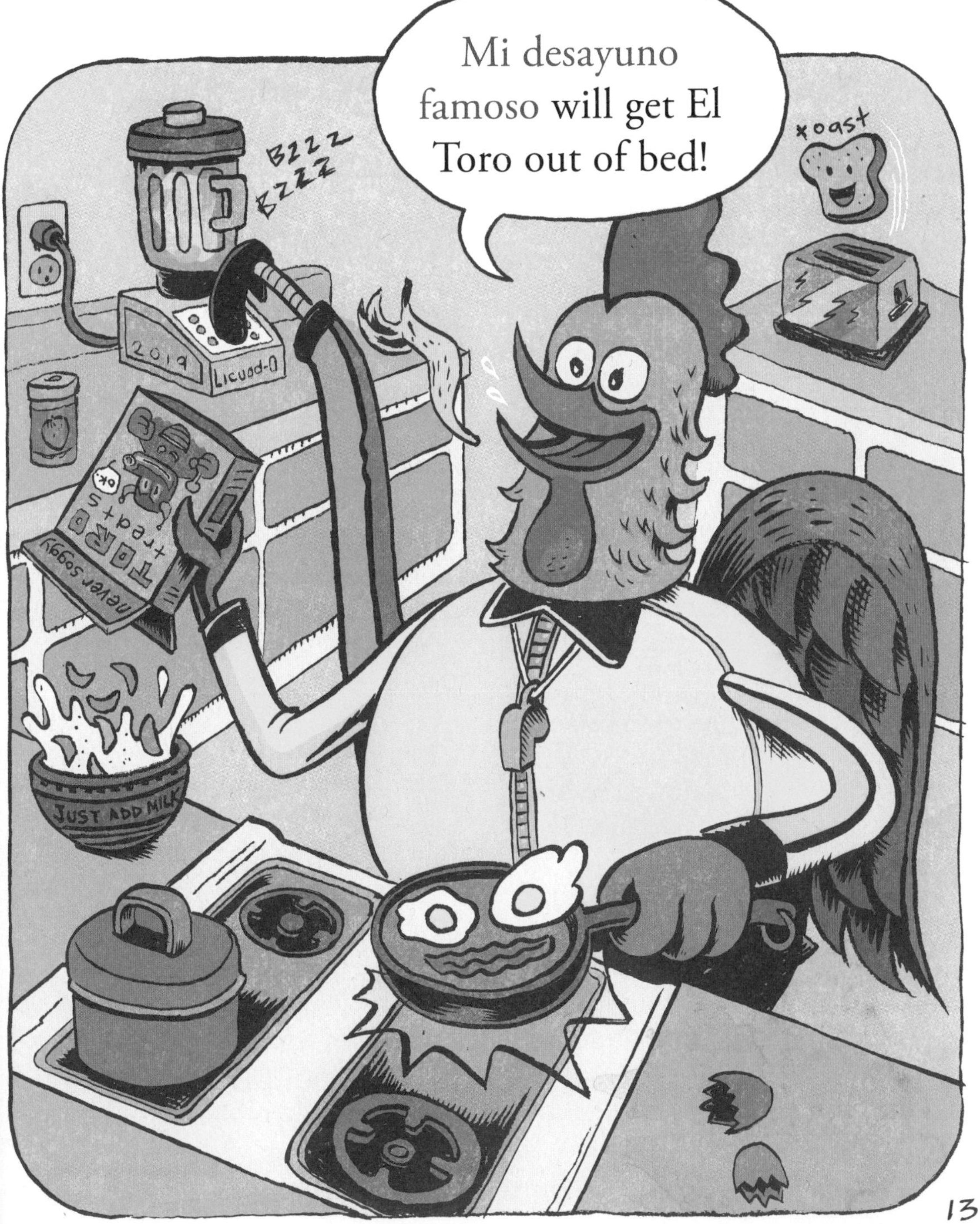
Mi desayuno famoso will get El Toro out of bed!
BZZZ BZZZ
toast
2019
Licuad-O
never soggy
TORO treats
ok.
JUST ADD MILK

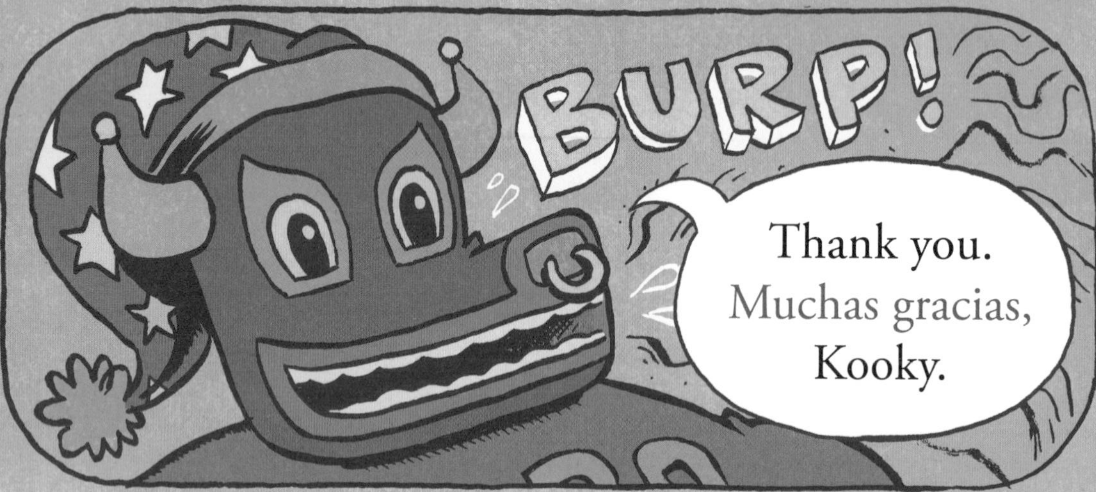
BURP!
Thank you.
Muchas gracias,
Kooky.

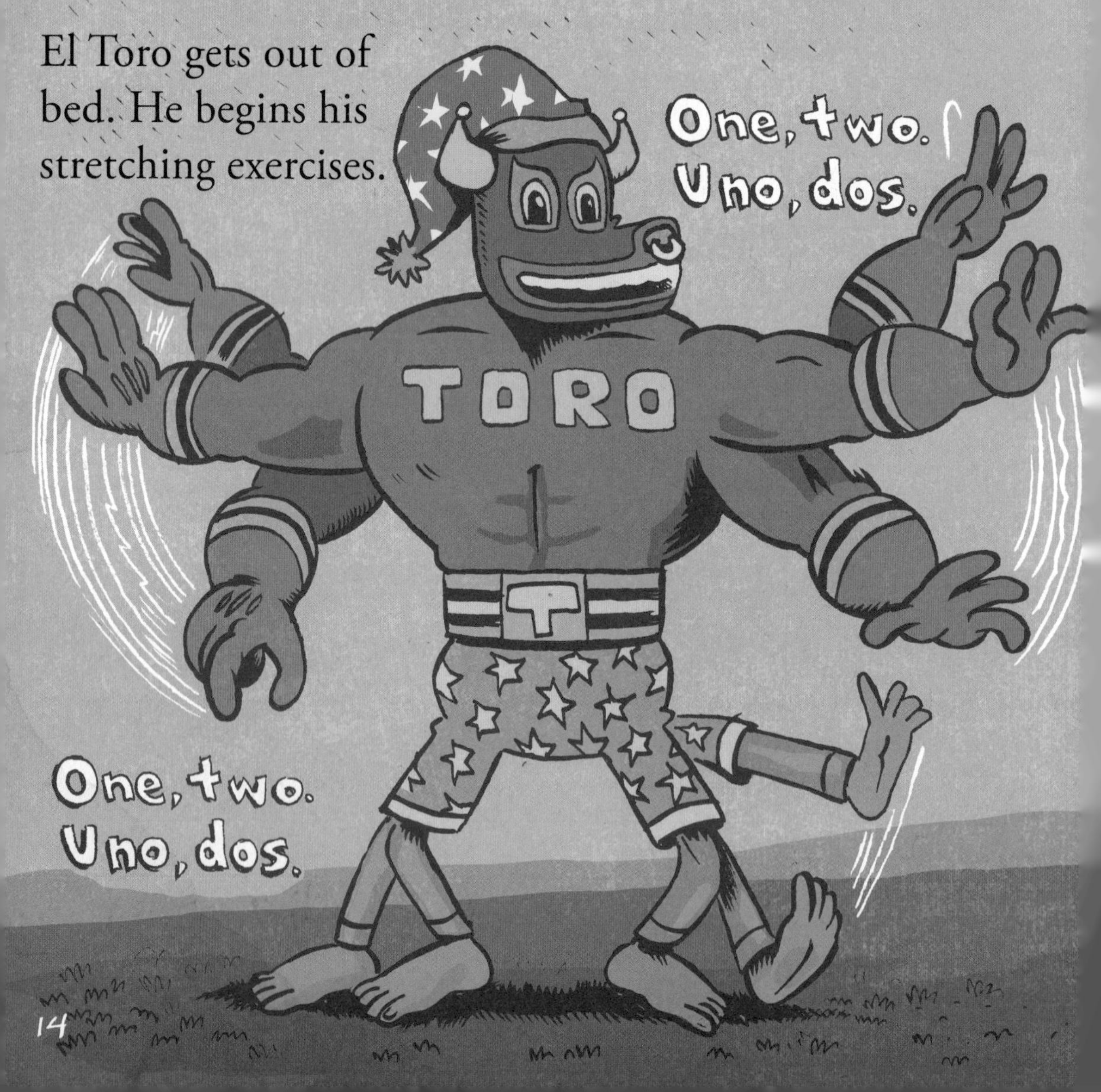
El Toro gets out of bed. He begins his stretching exercises.
One, two.
Uno, dos.
TORO
One, two.
Uno, dos.

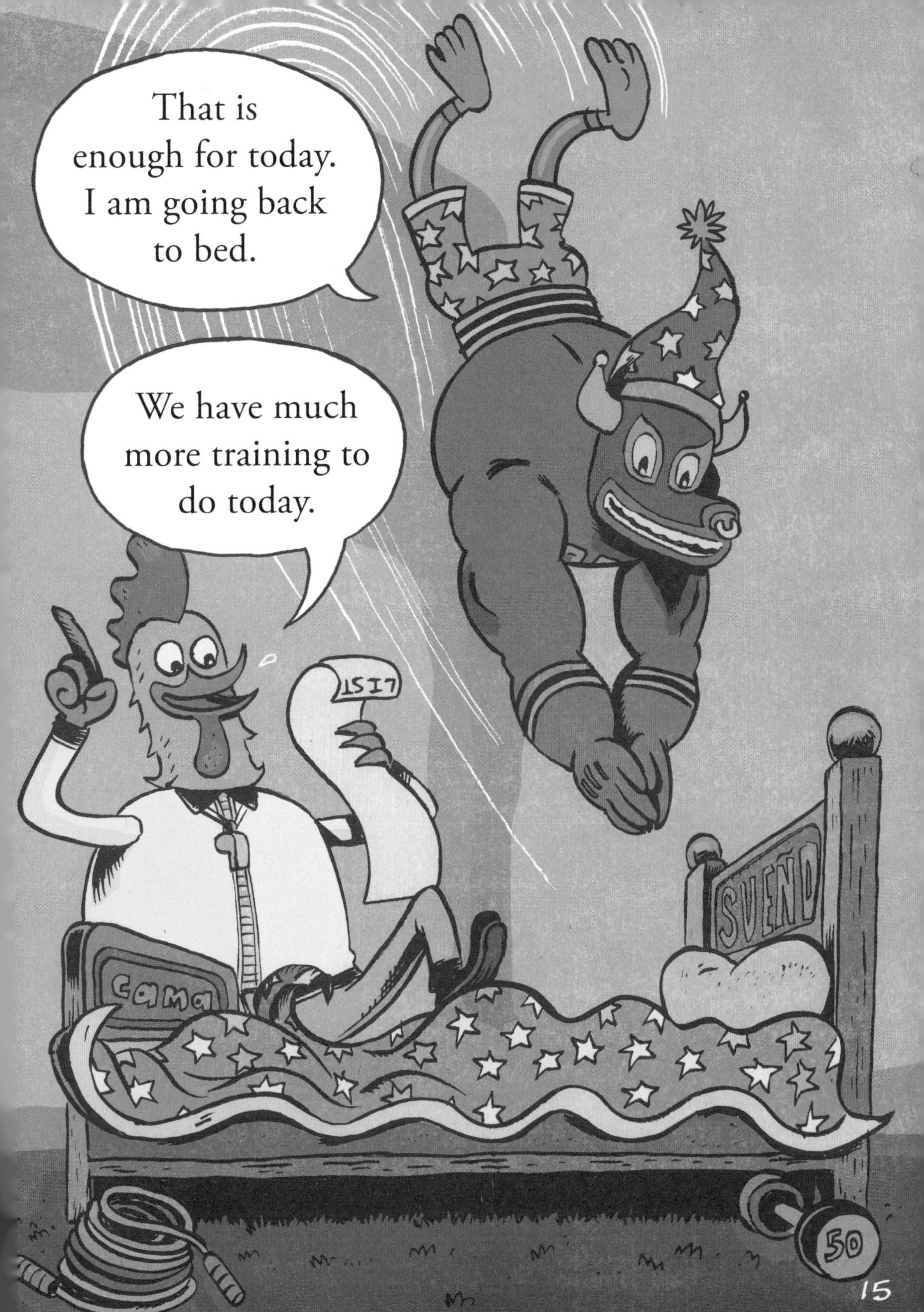
That is enough for today. I am going back to bed.
We have much more training to do today.
SUEÑO
cama
50

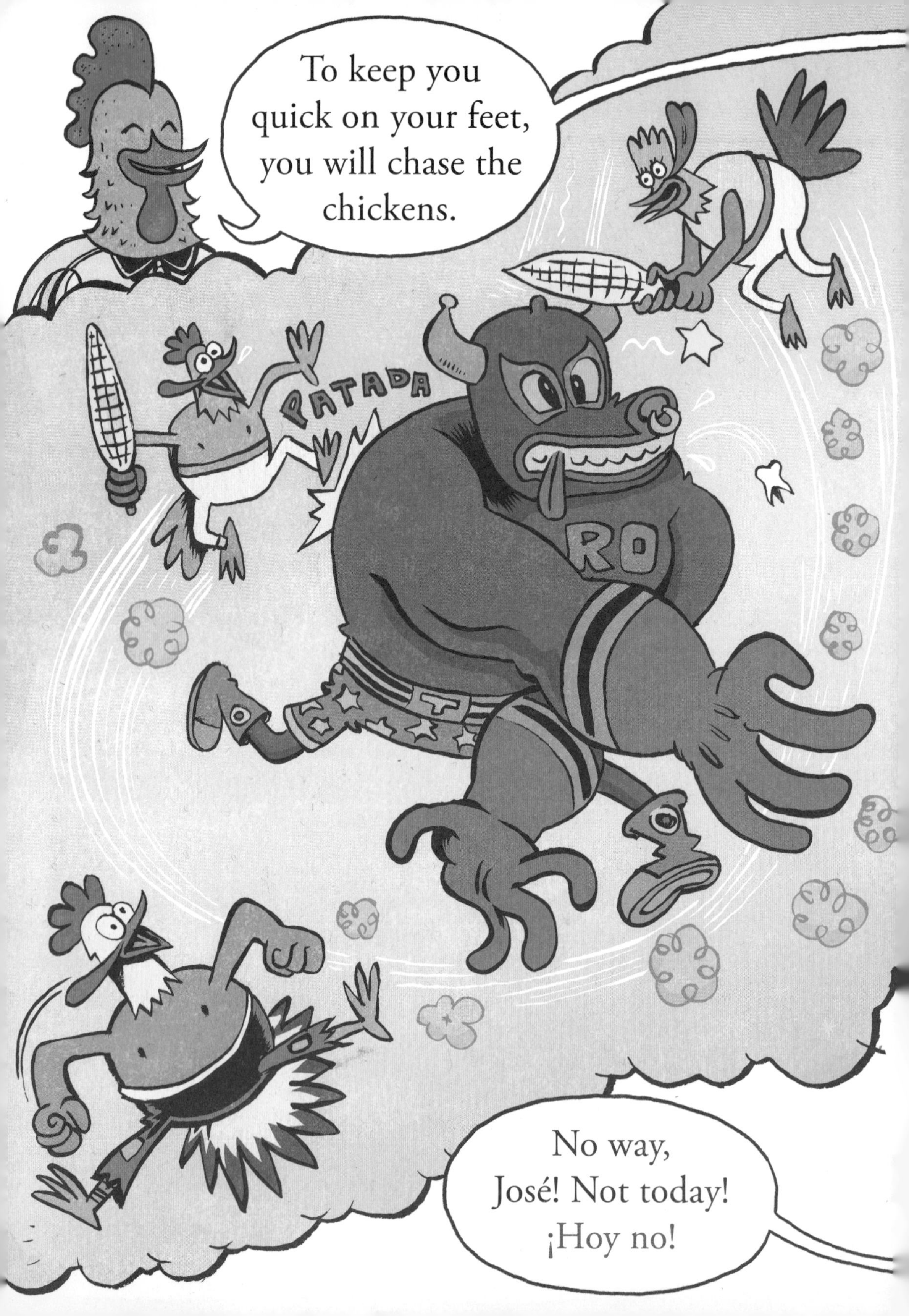
To keep you quick on your feet, you will chase the chickens.
PATADA
RO
No way, José! Not today! ¡Hoy no!

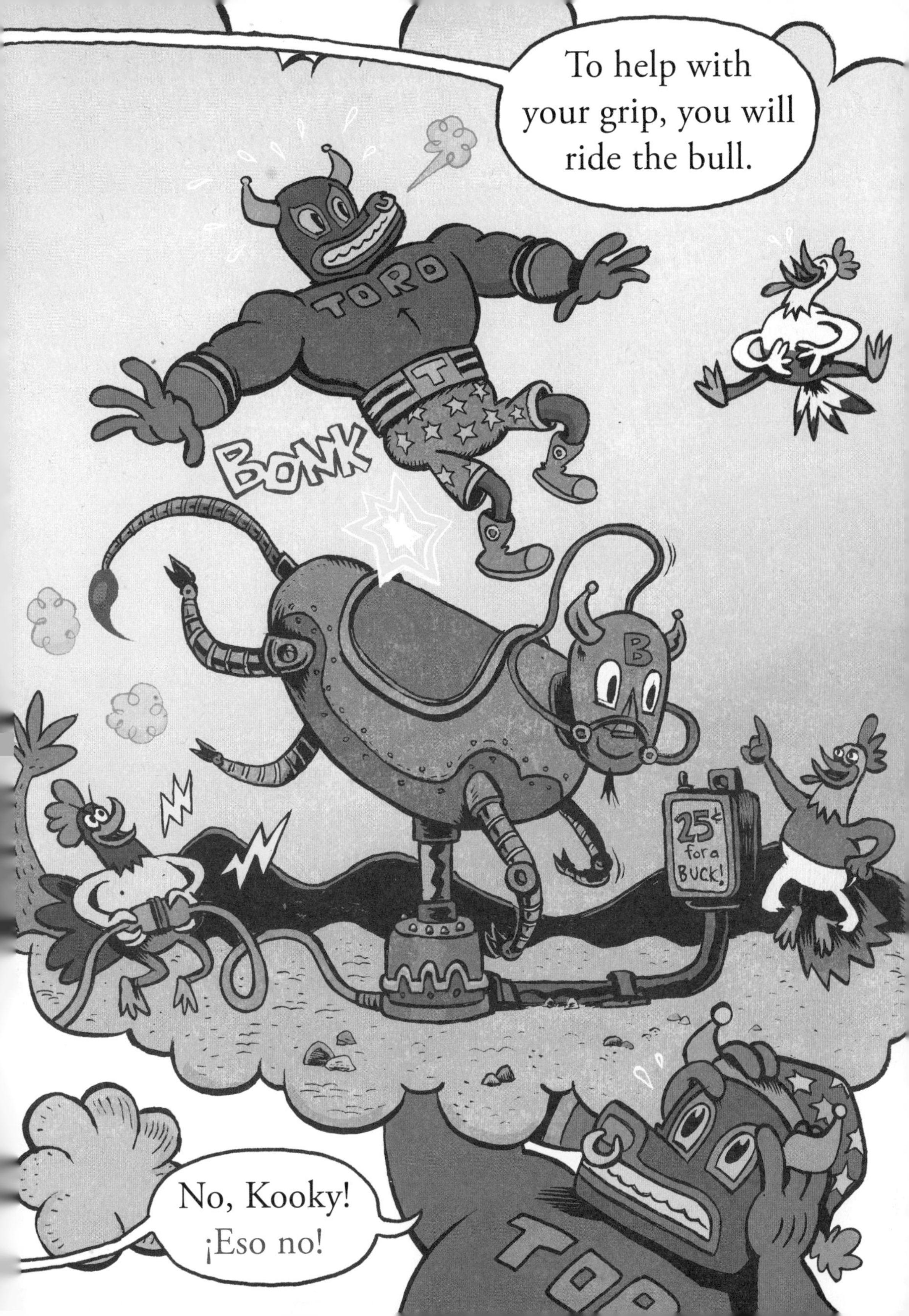
To help with your grip, you will ride the bull.
TORO
T
BONK
B
25¢ for a BUCK!
No, Kooky! ¡Eso no!
TOR

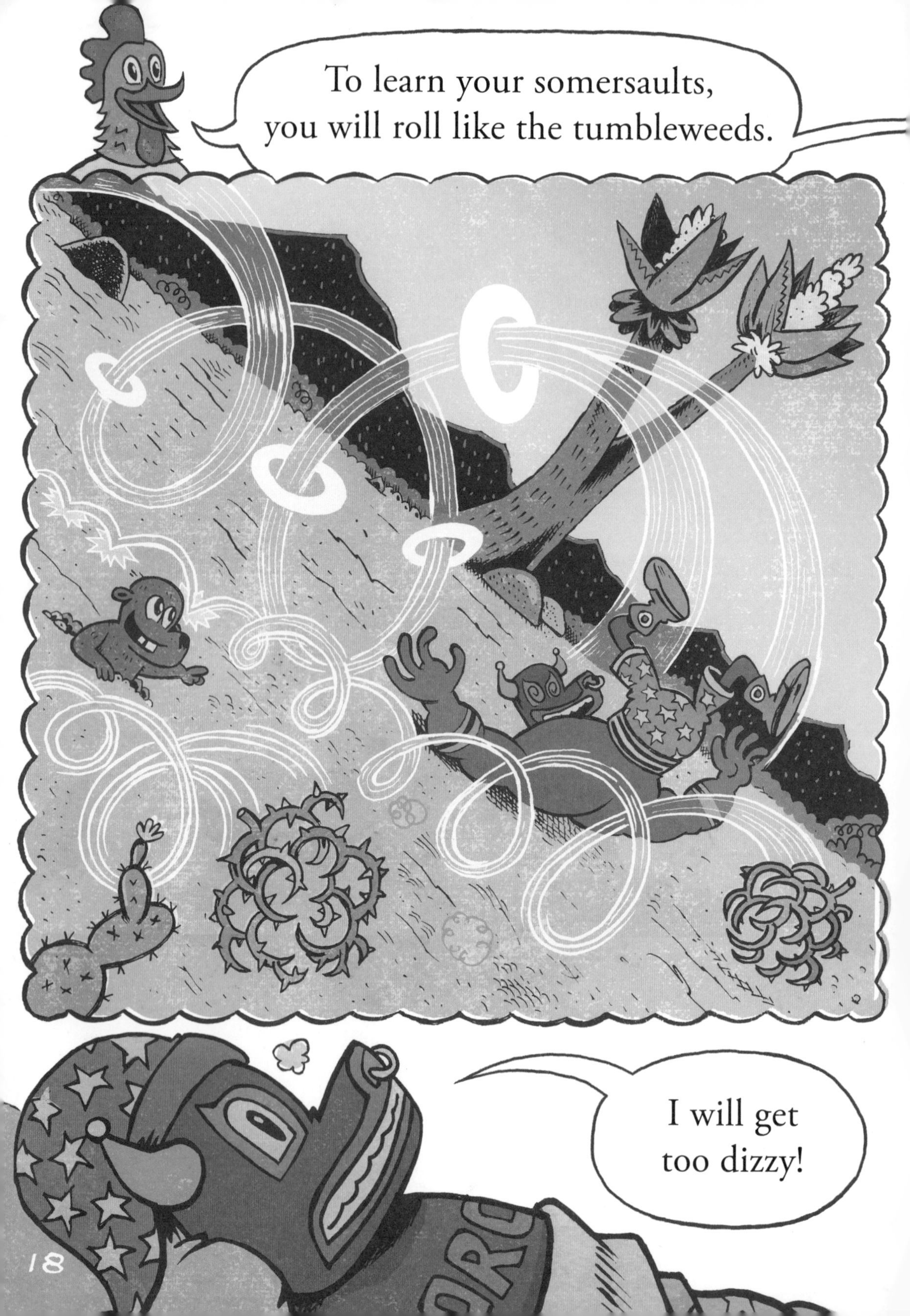
To learn your somersaults,
you will roll like the tumbleweeds.
I will get
too dizzy!

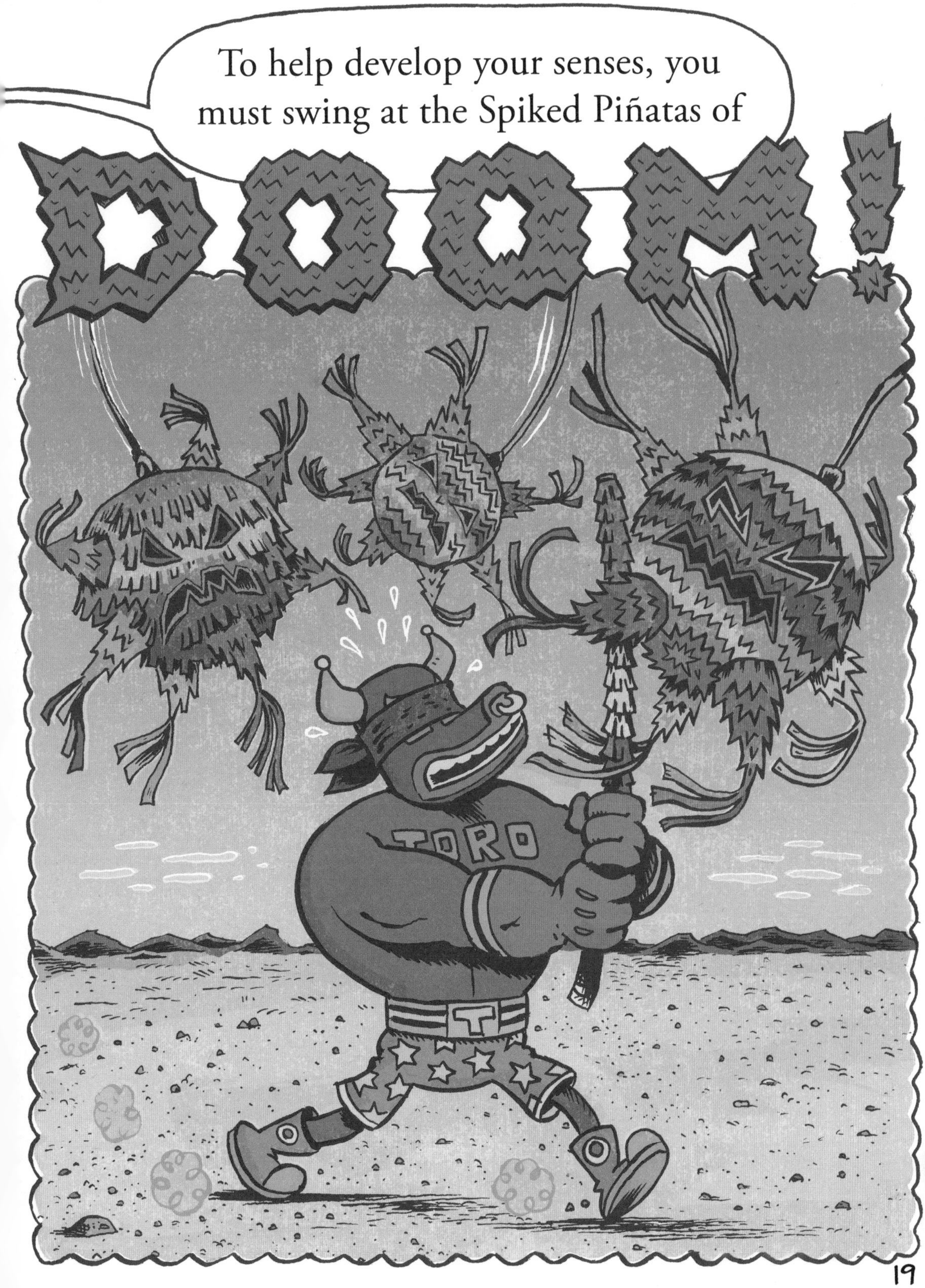
To help develop your senses, you must swing at the Spiked Piñatas of
DOOM!
TORO
T

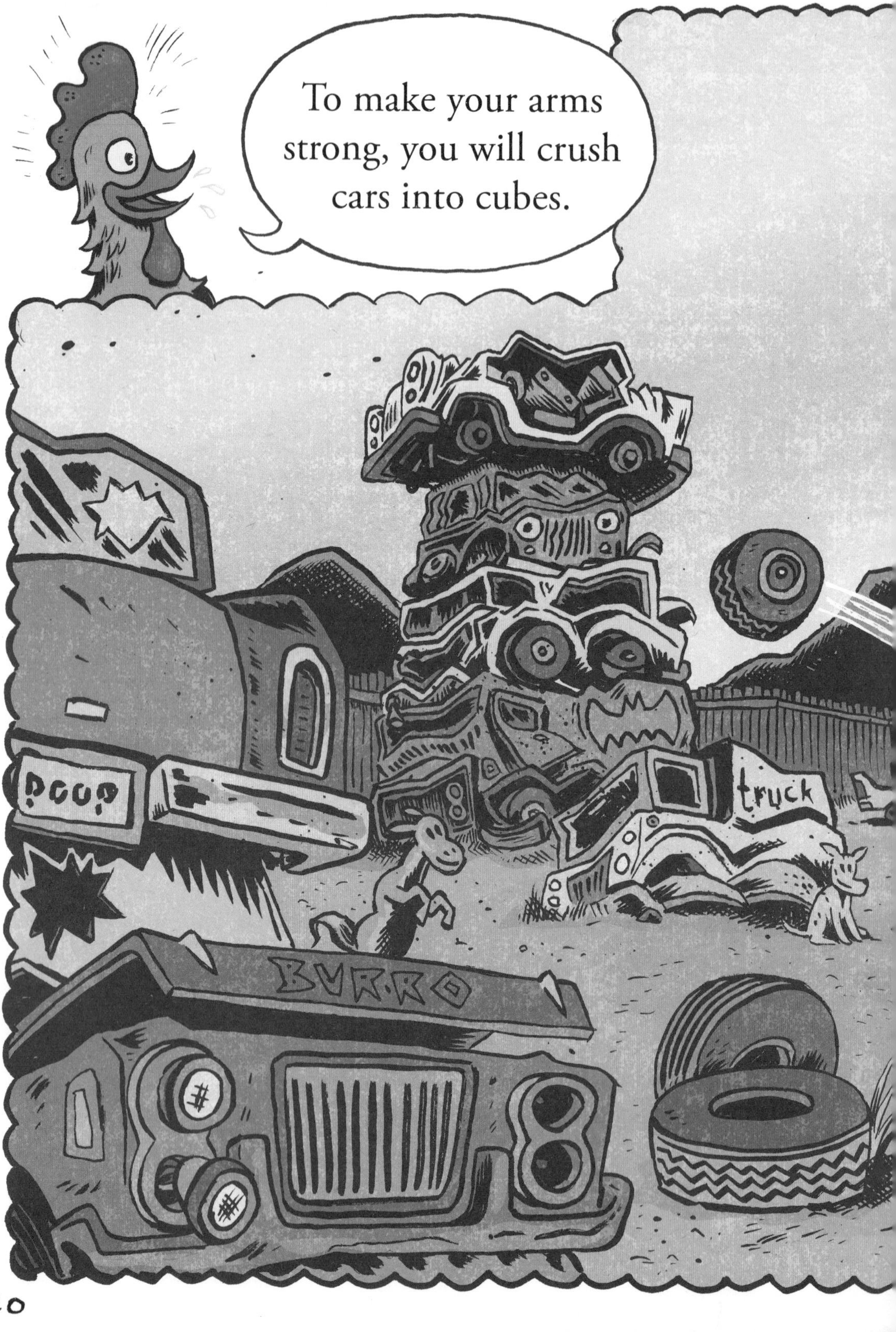
To make your arms strong, you will crush cars into cubes.
BURRO
truck

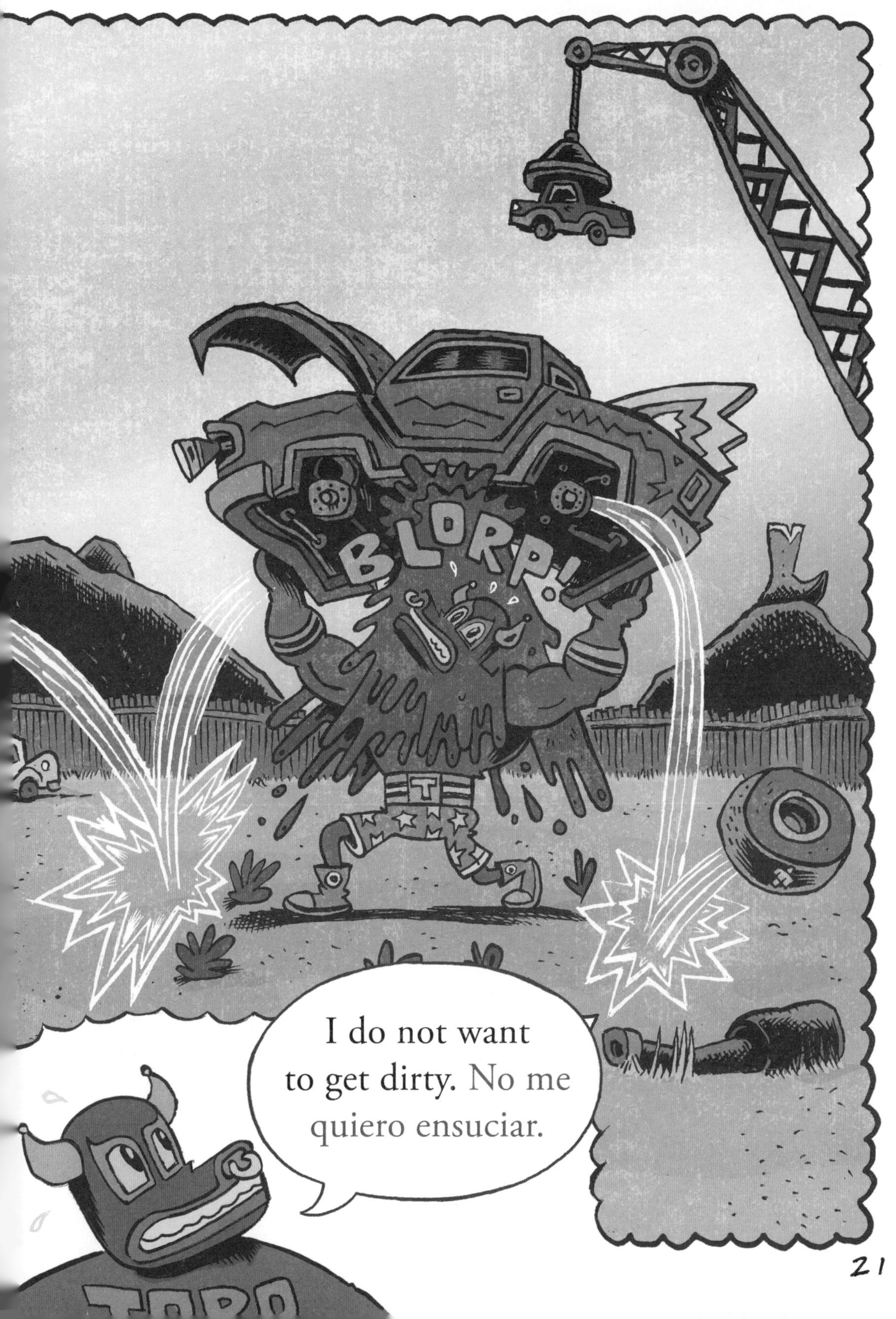
BLORP!
I do not want to get dirty. No me quiero ensuciar.

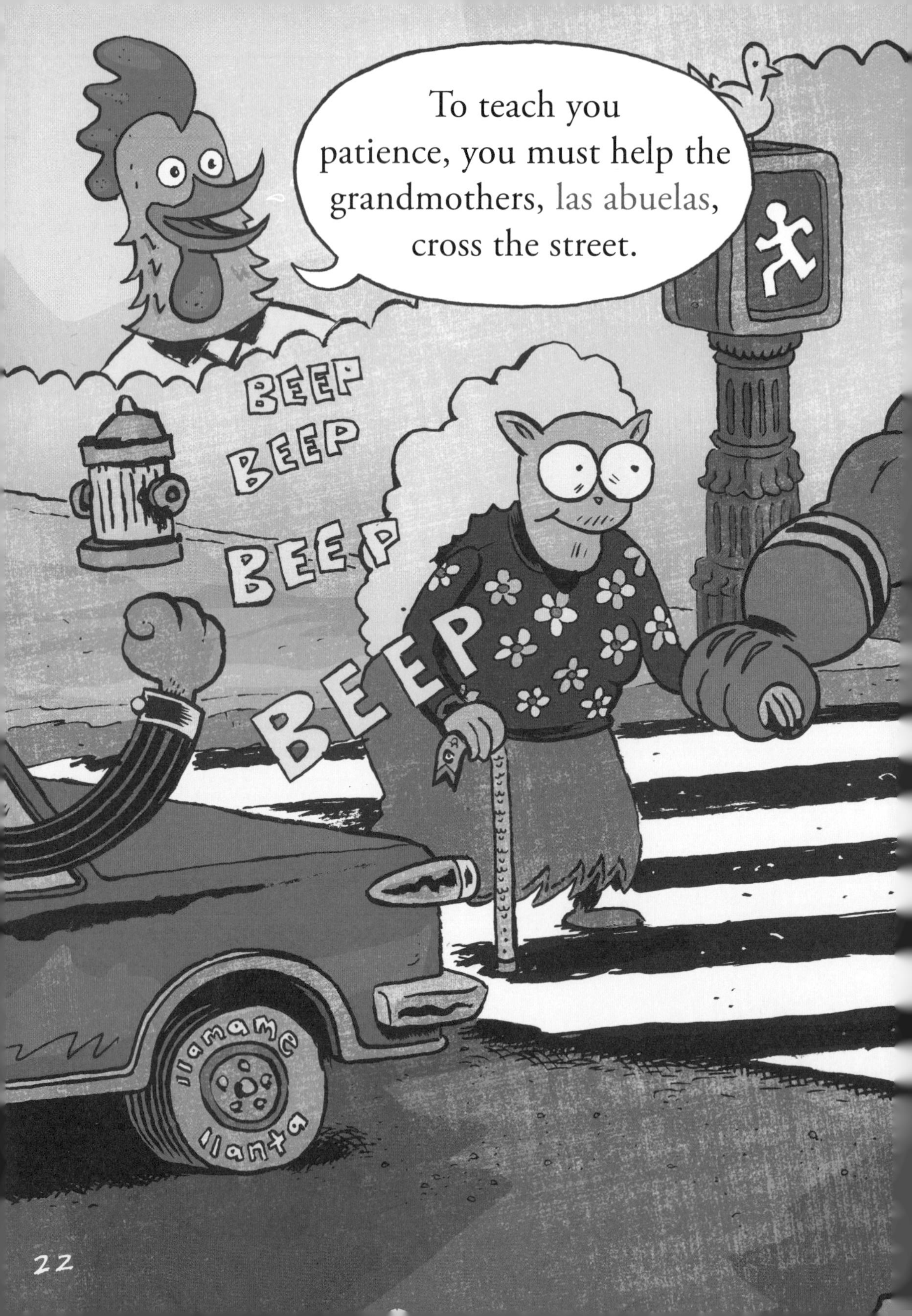
To teach you patience, you must help the grandmothers, las abuelas, cross the street.
BEEP
BEEP
BEEP
BEEP
llamame
llanta

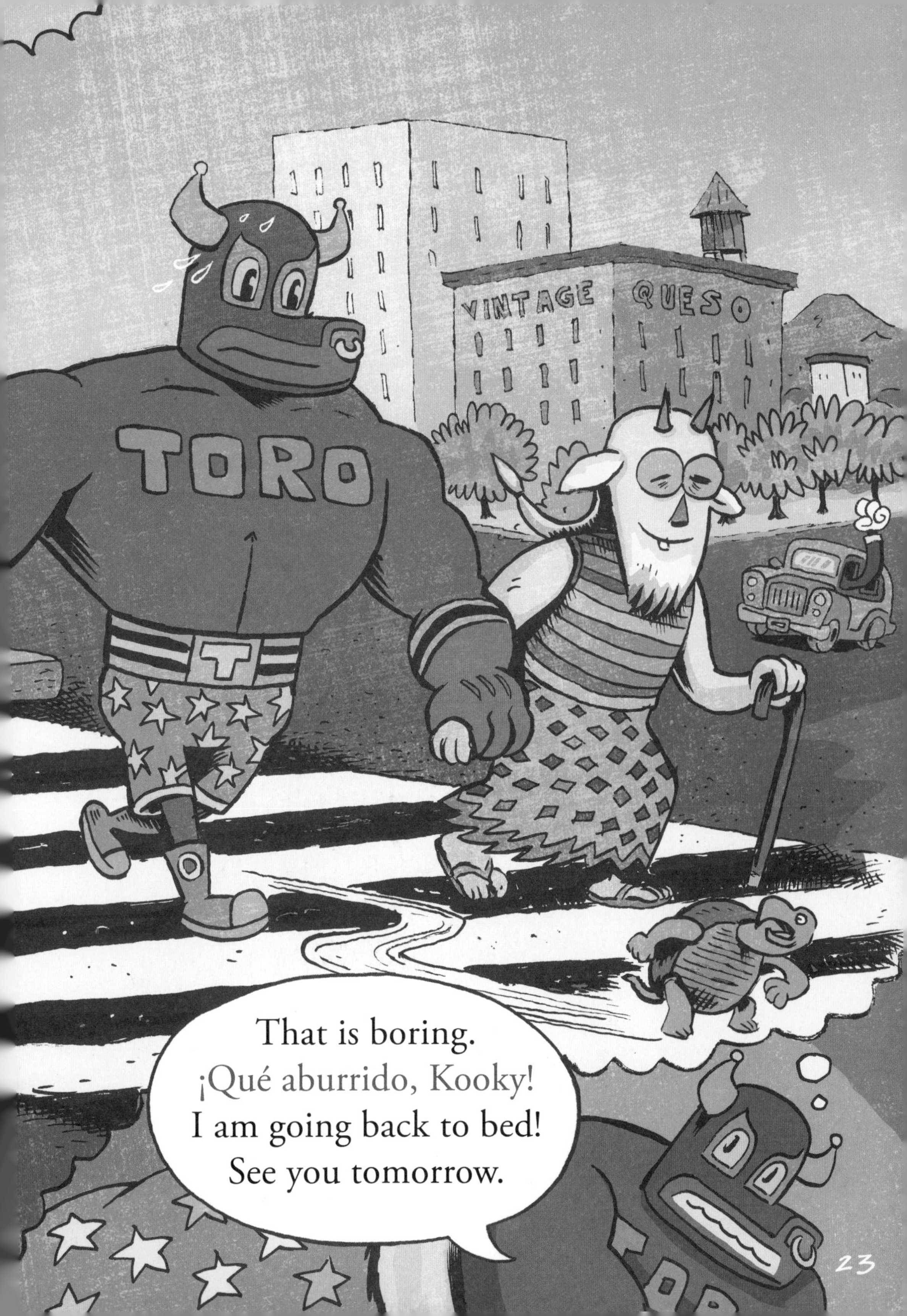
VINTAGE QUESO
TORO
That is boring.
¡Qué aburrido, Kooky!
I am going back to bed!
See you tomorrow.

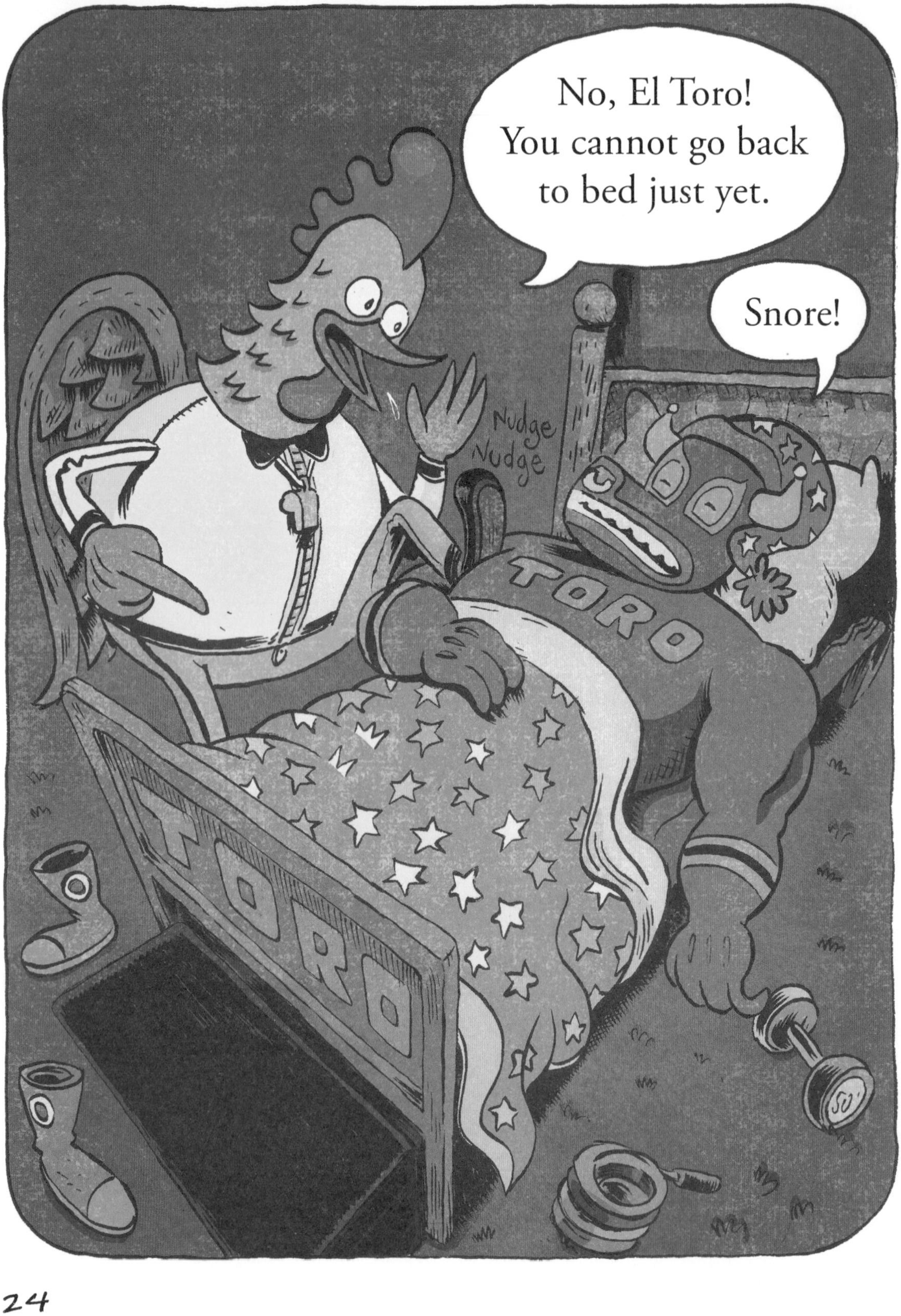
No, El Toro!
You cannot go back
to bed just yet.
Snore!
Nudge
Nudge
TORO
TORO

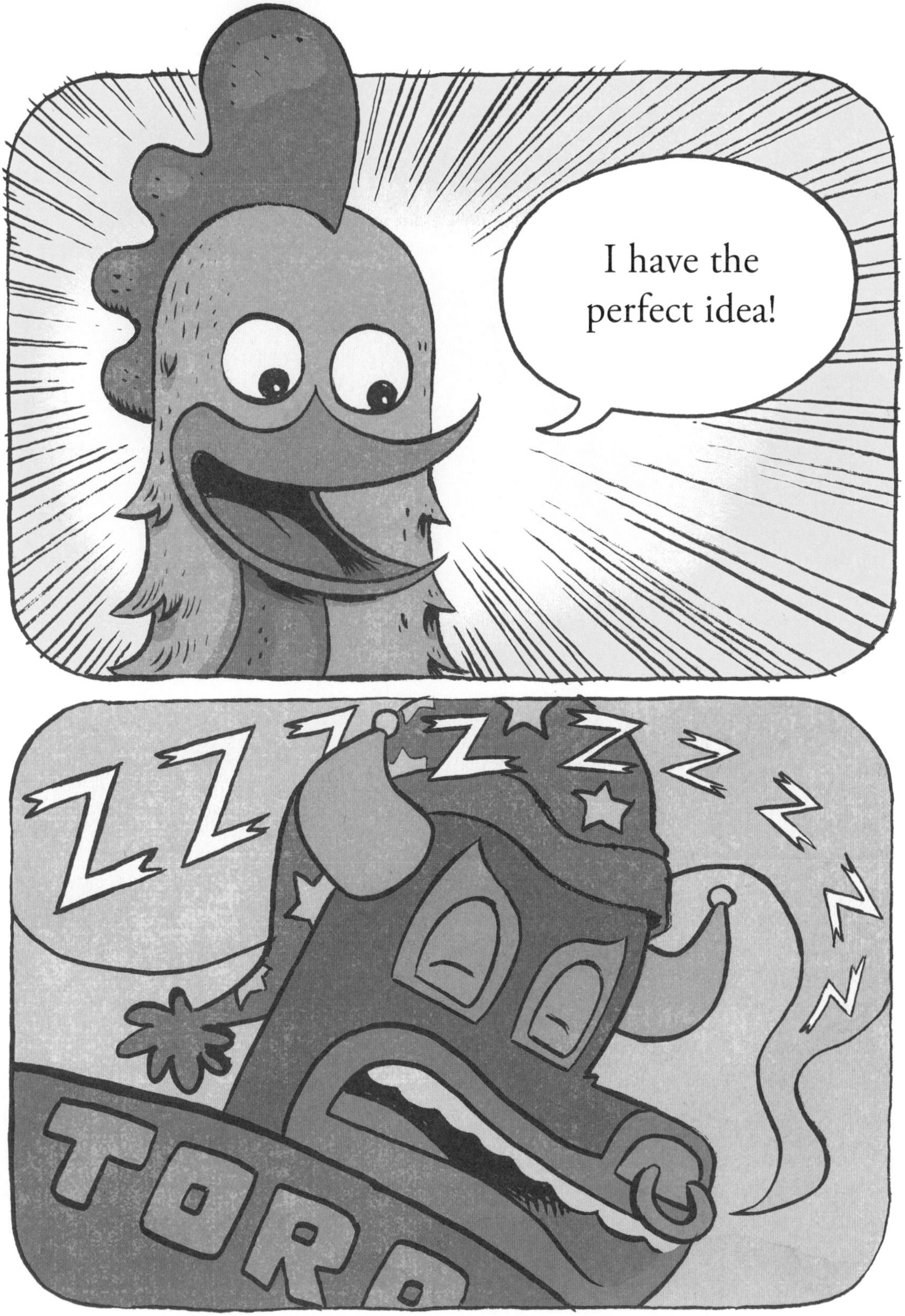
I have the perfect idea!

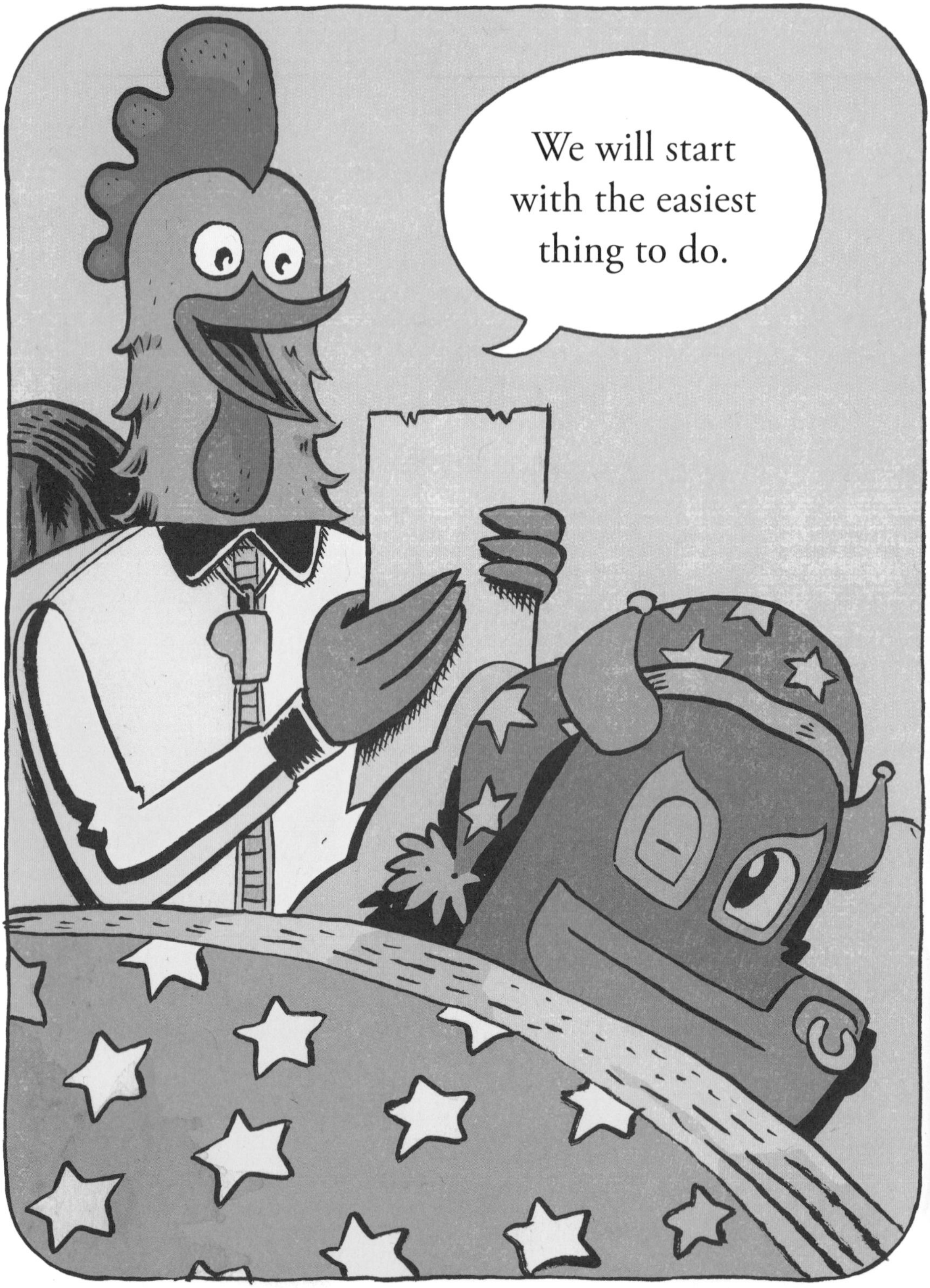
We will start with the easiest thing to do.

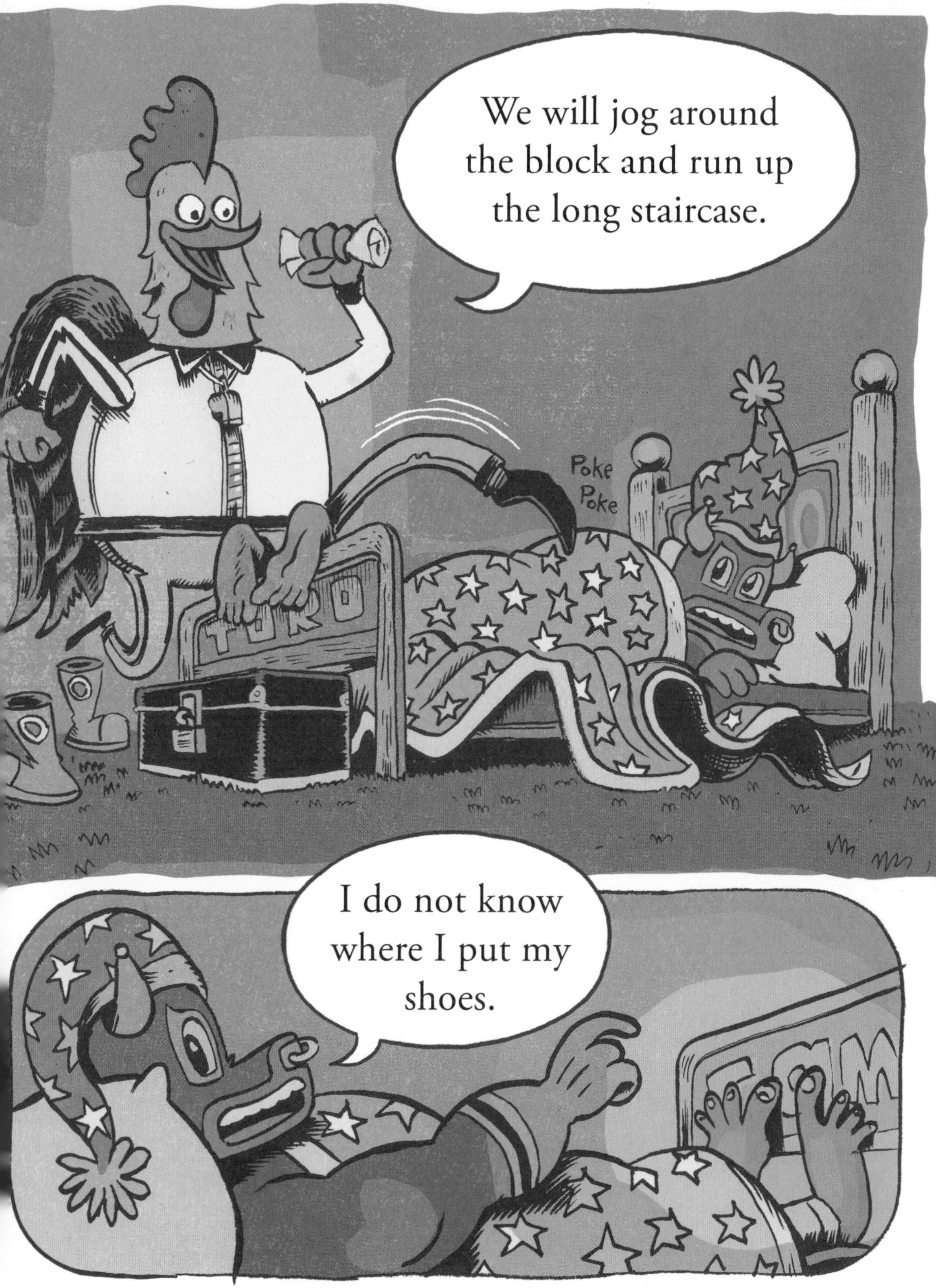
We will jog around the block and run up the long staircase.
Poke Poke
TORO
I do not know where I put my shoes.

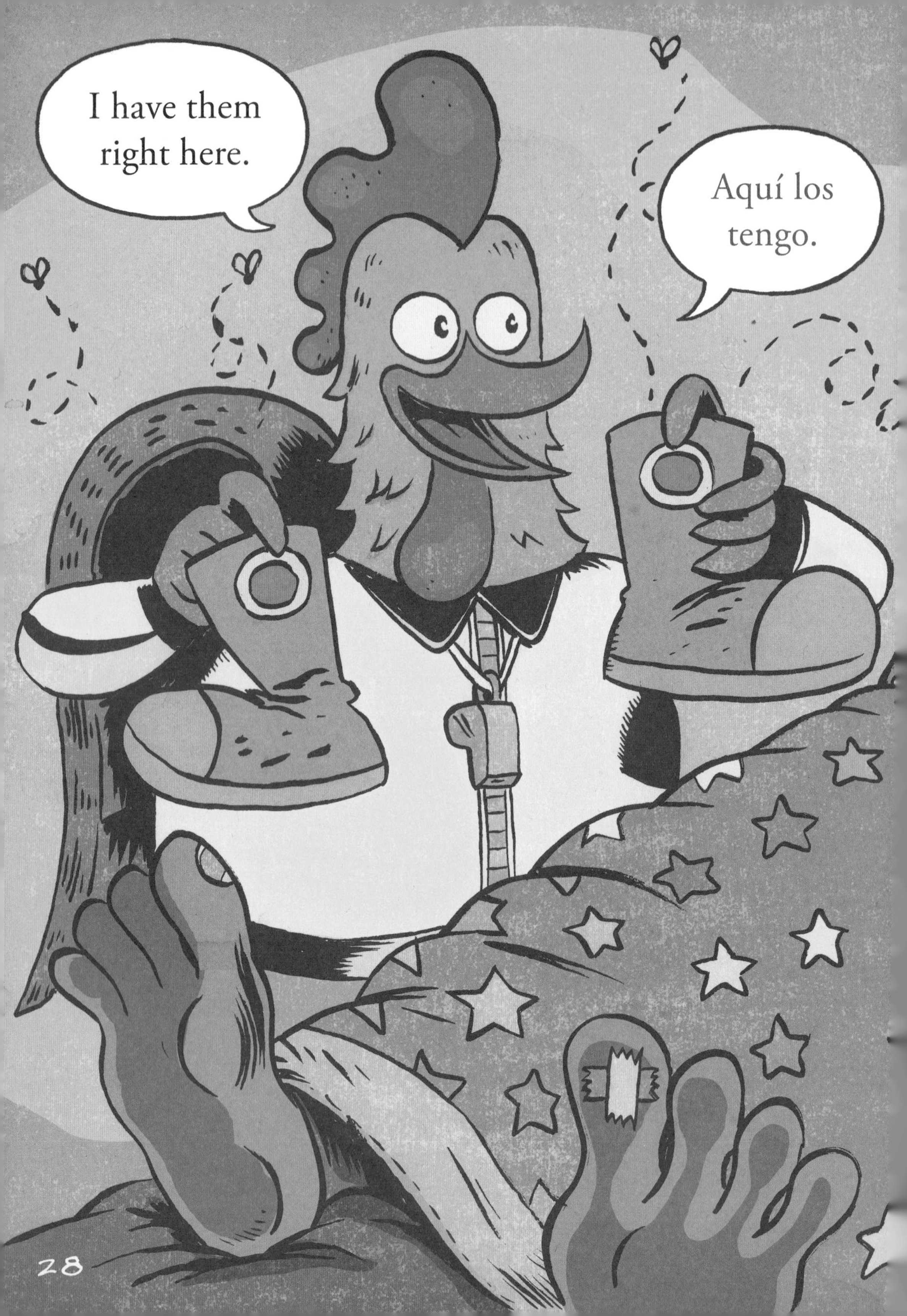
I have them right here.
Aquí los tengo.

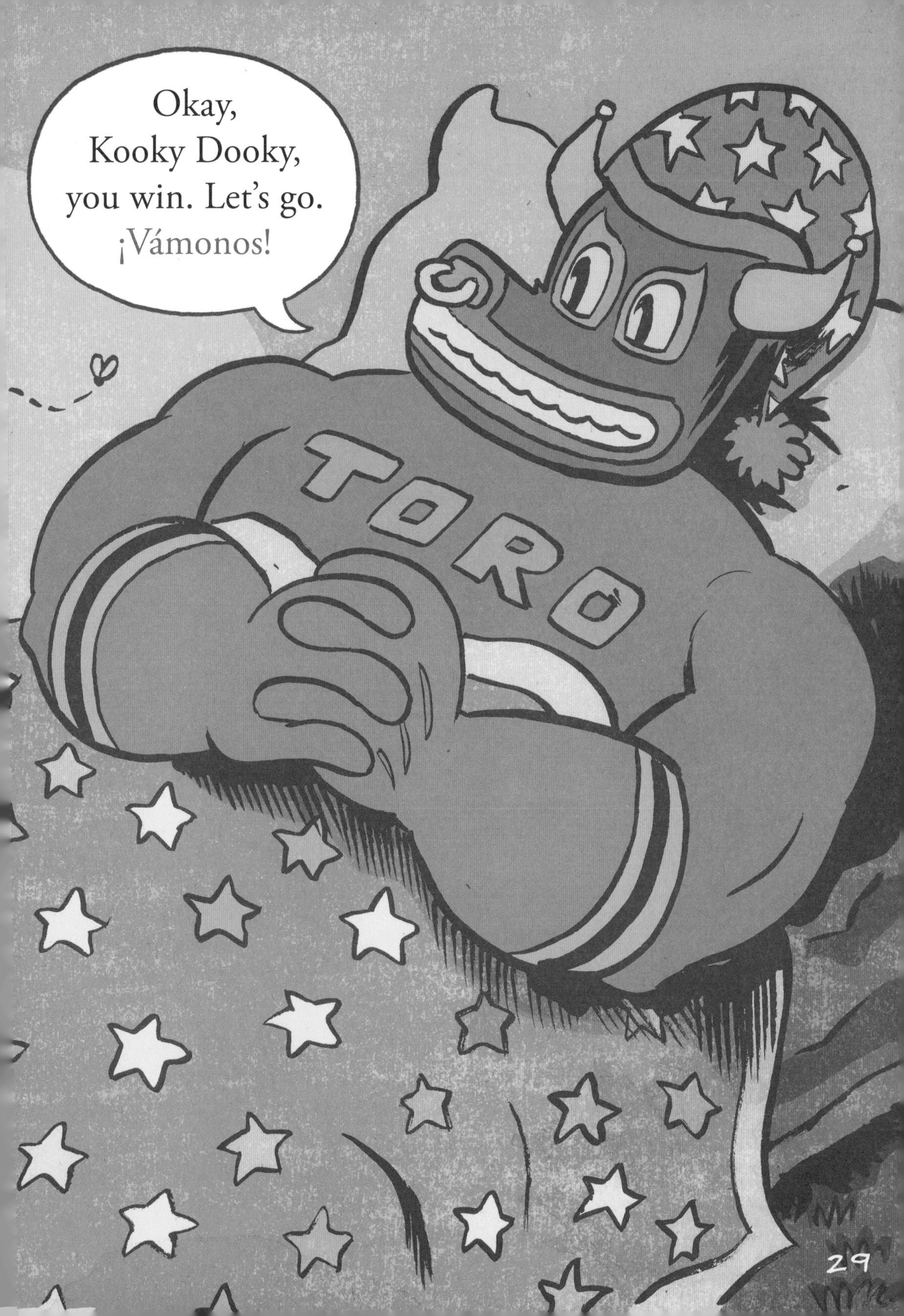
Okay, Kooky Dooky, you win. Let's go. ¡Vámonos!
TORO

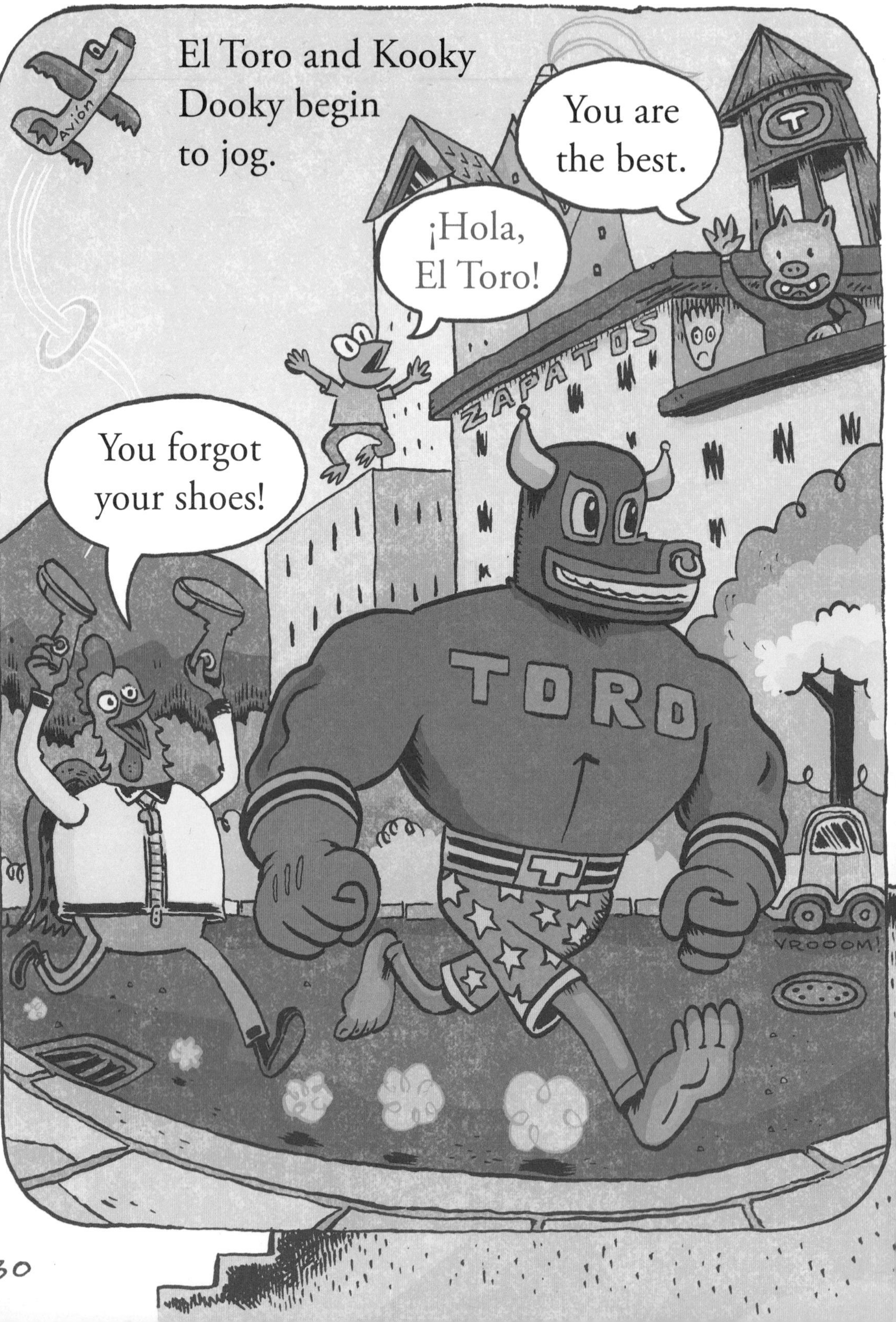
El Toro and Kooky Dooky begin to jog.
Avión
You are the best.
¡Hola, El Toro!
ZAPATOS
You forgot your shoes!
TORO
VROOOM!

El Toro speeds up and begins climbing the stairs.

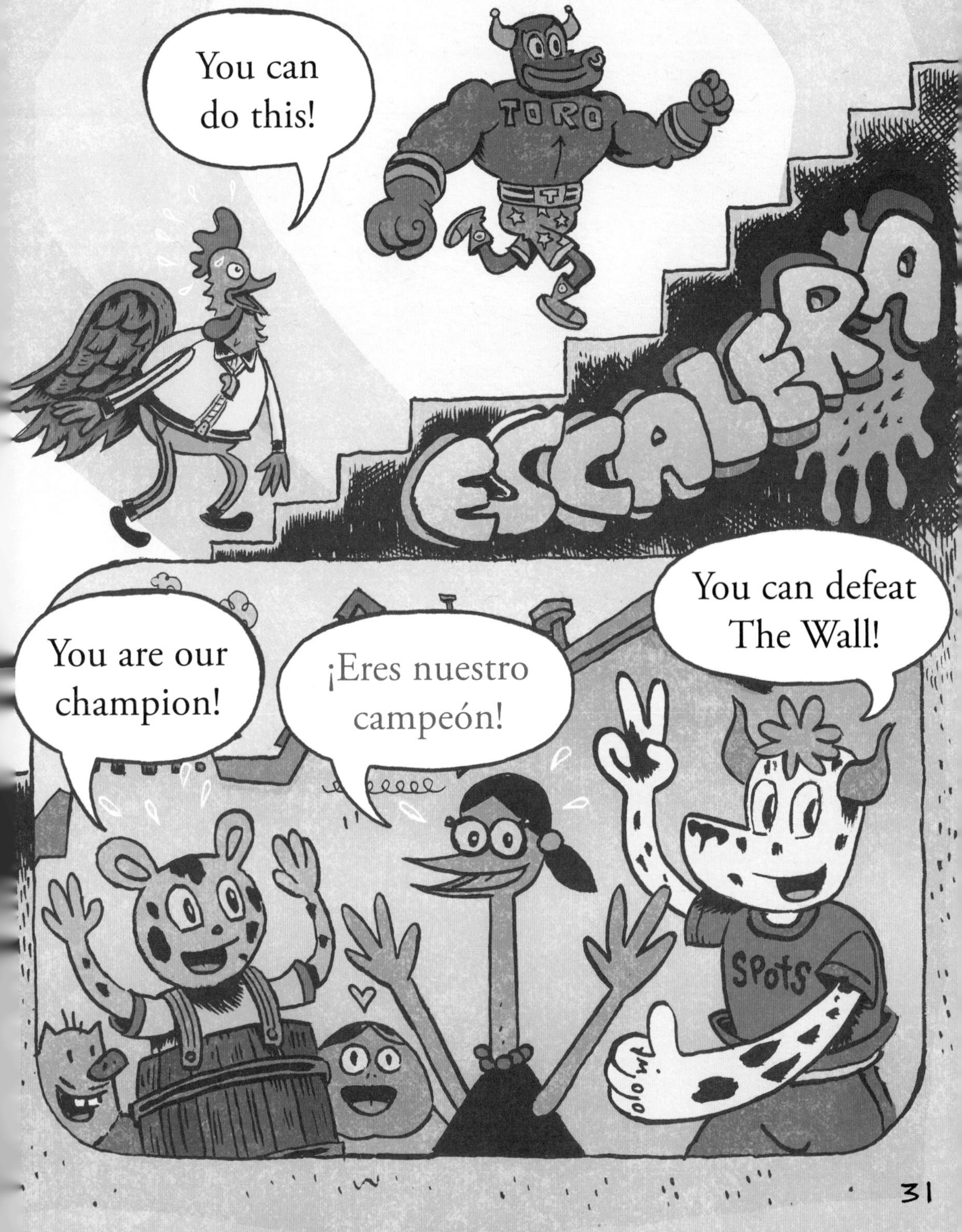
You can do this!
TORO
ESCALERA
You are our champion!
¡Eres nuestro campeón!
You can defeat The Wall!
SPOTS

El Toro feels inspired
by the love of his fans.

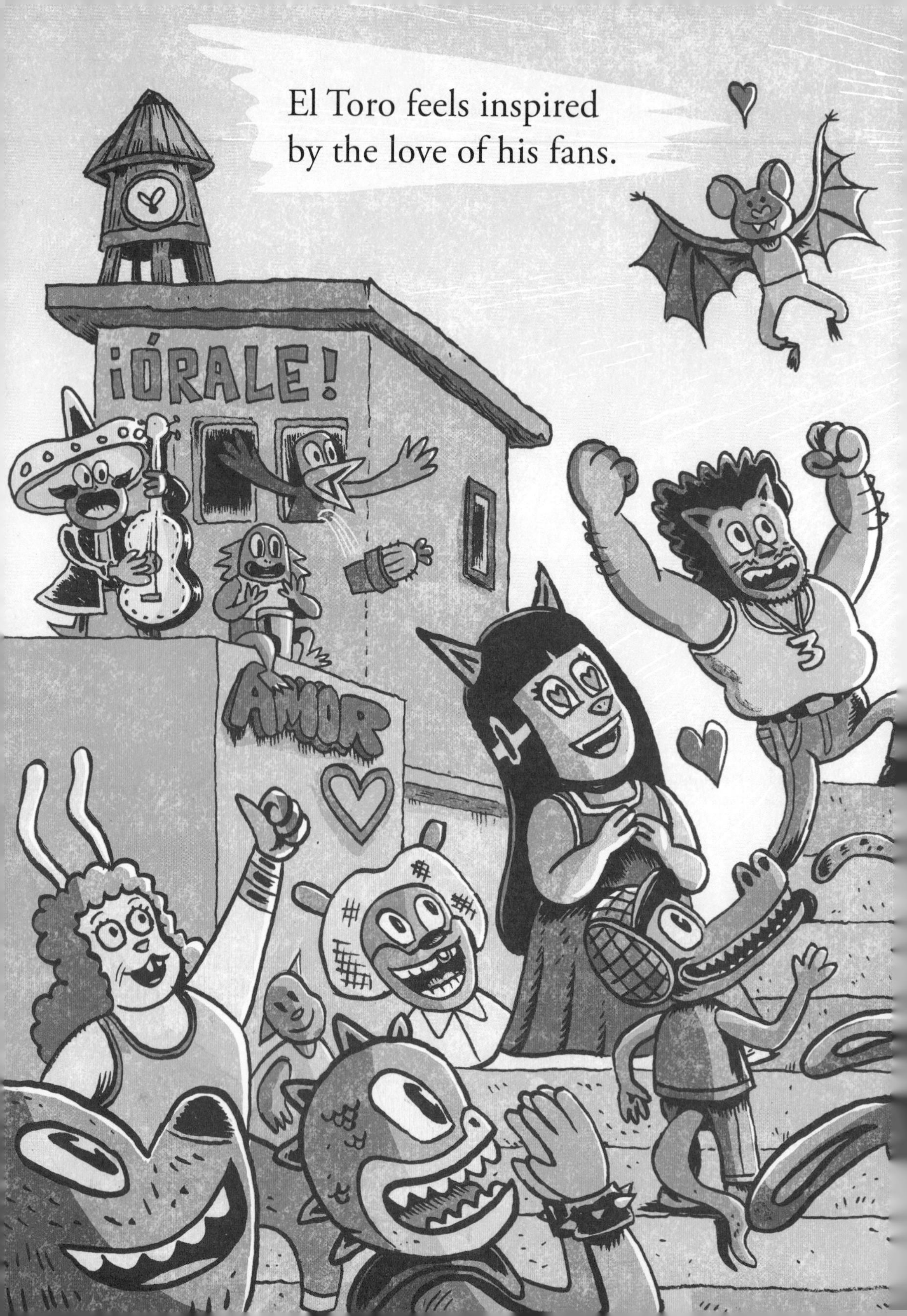
¡ÓRALE!
AMOR

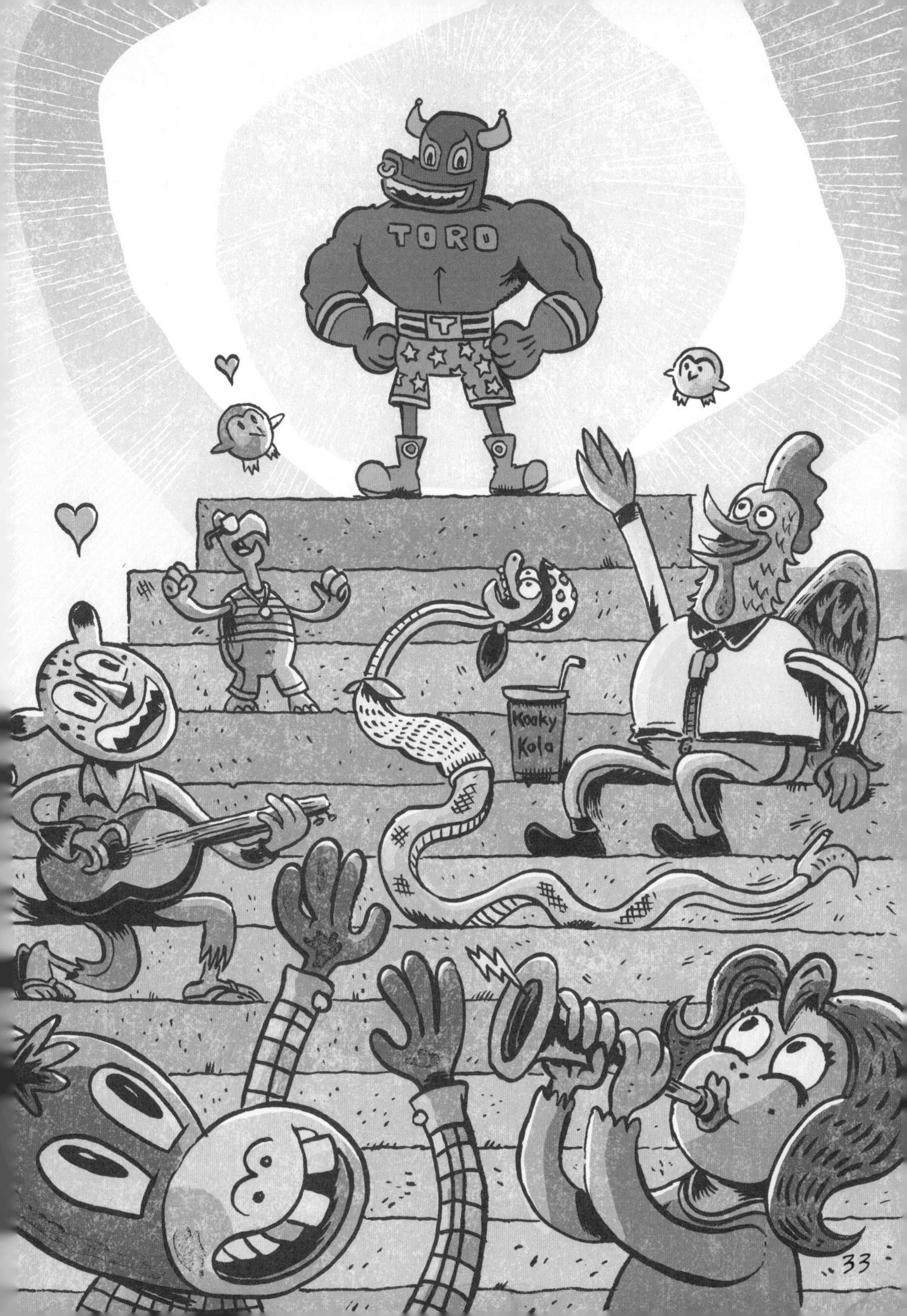
TORO
T
Kooky Kola

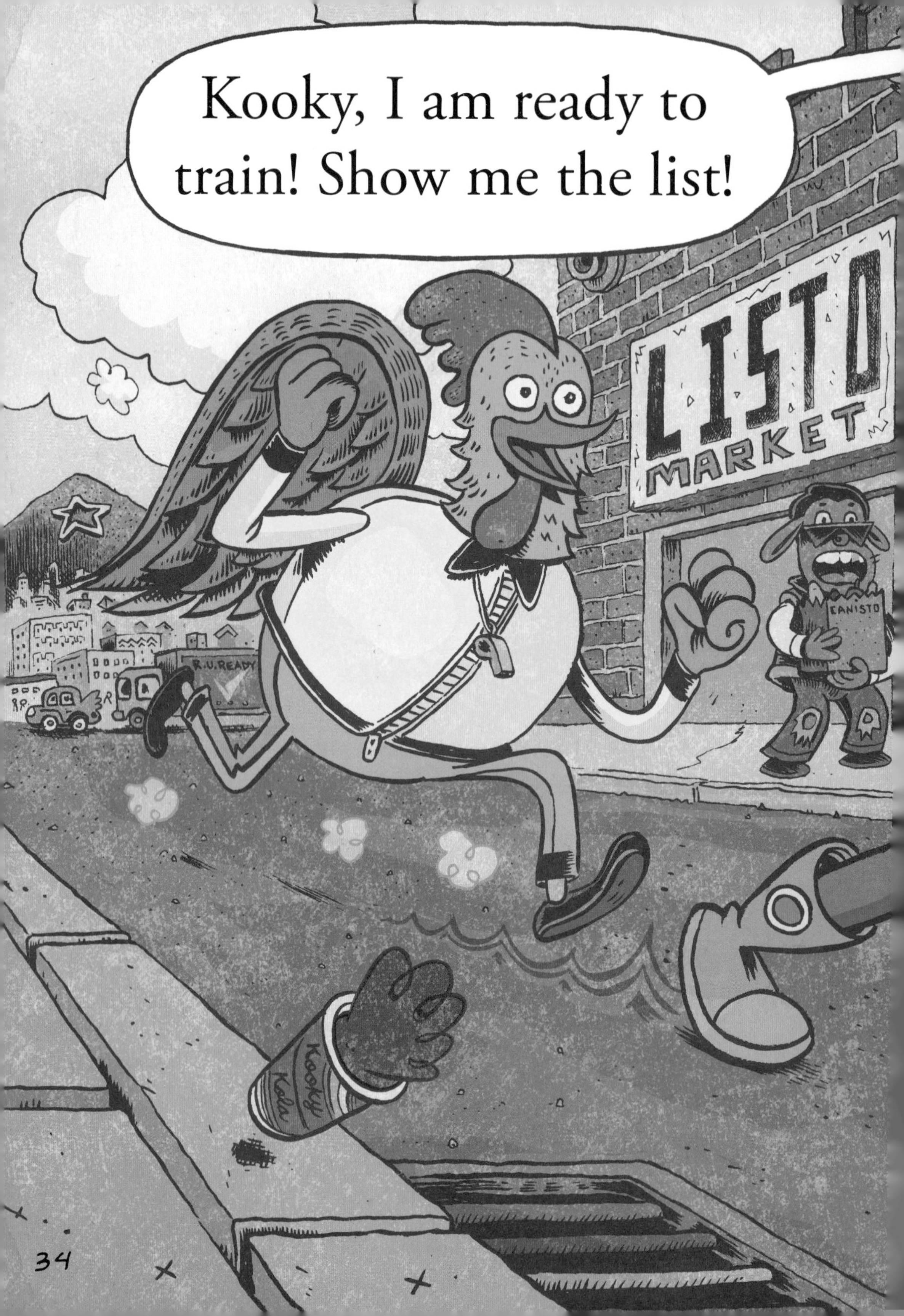
Kooky, I am ready to train! Show me the list!
LISTO MARKET
R.U. READY
CANISTO
Kooky Kola

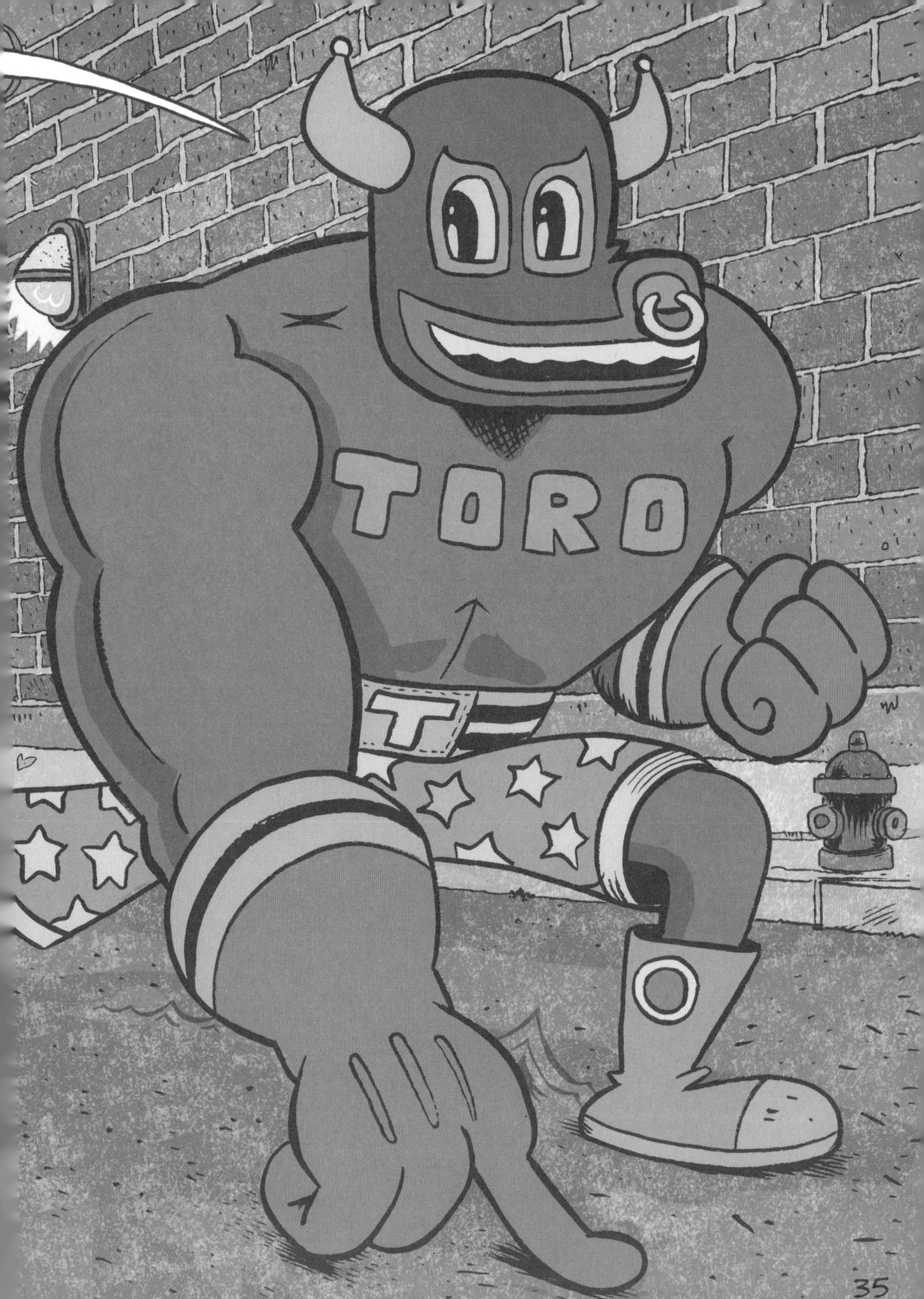
TORO
T

El Toro catches the chickens.

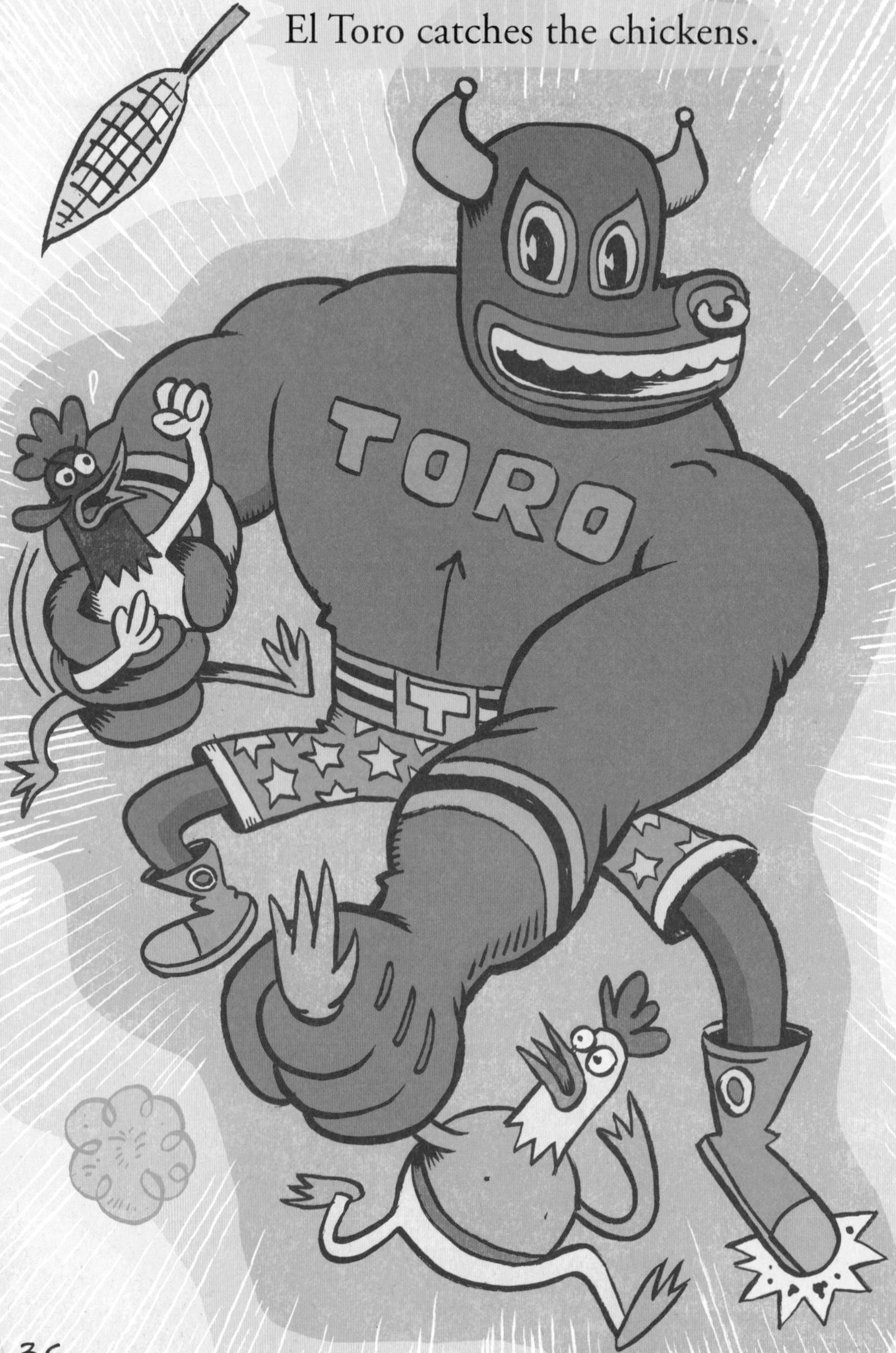
TORO
T

He rides the bull!

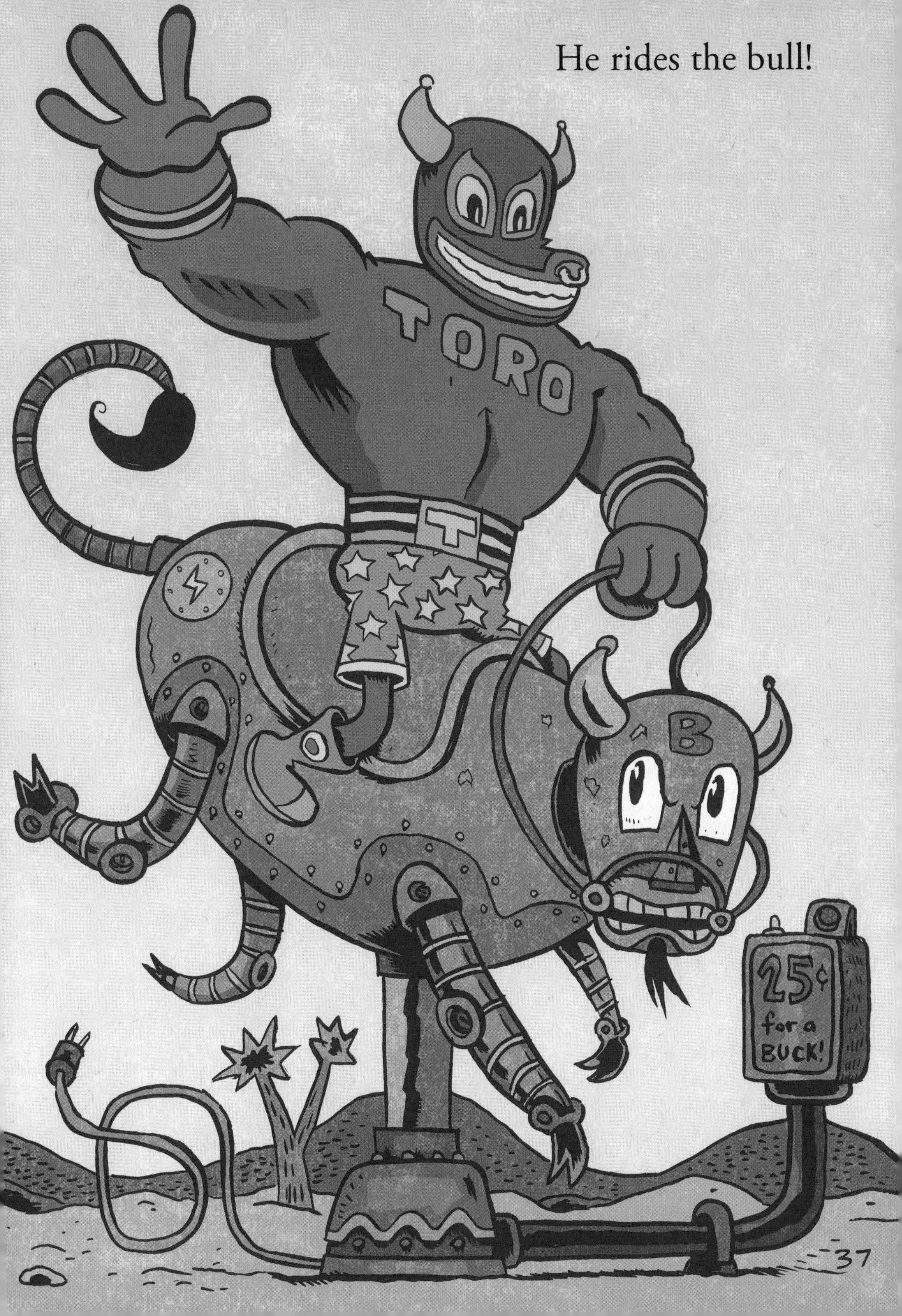
TORO
T
B
25¢
for a
BUCK!

He rolls like the tumbleweeds

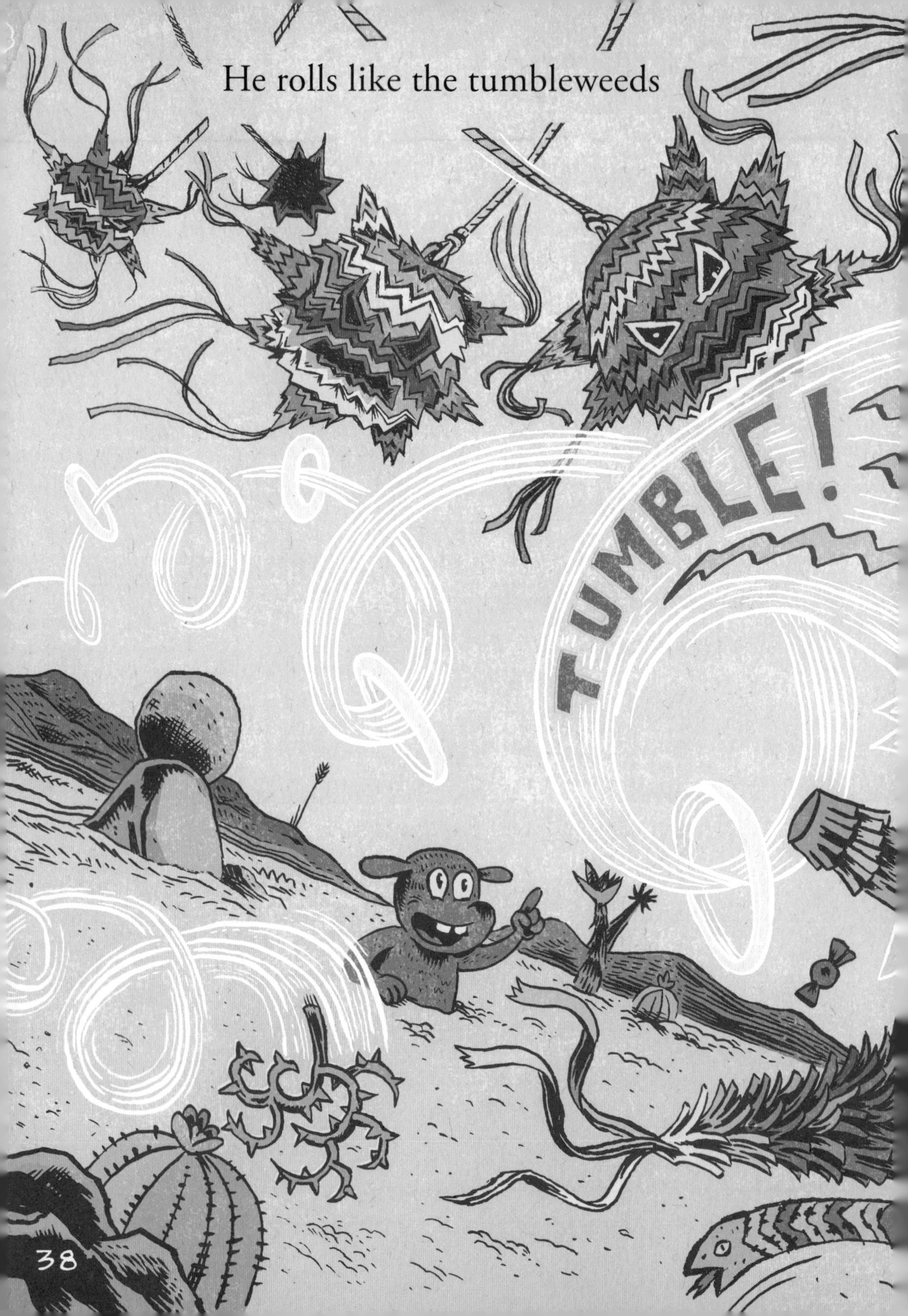
TUMBLE!

and smashes the piñatas!

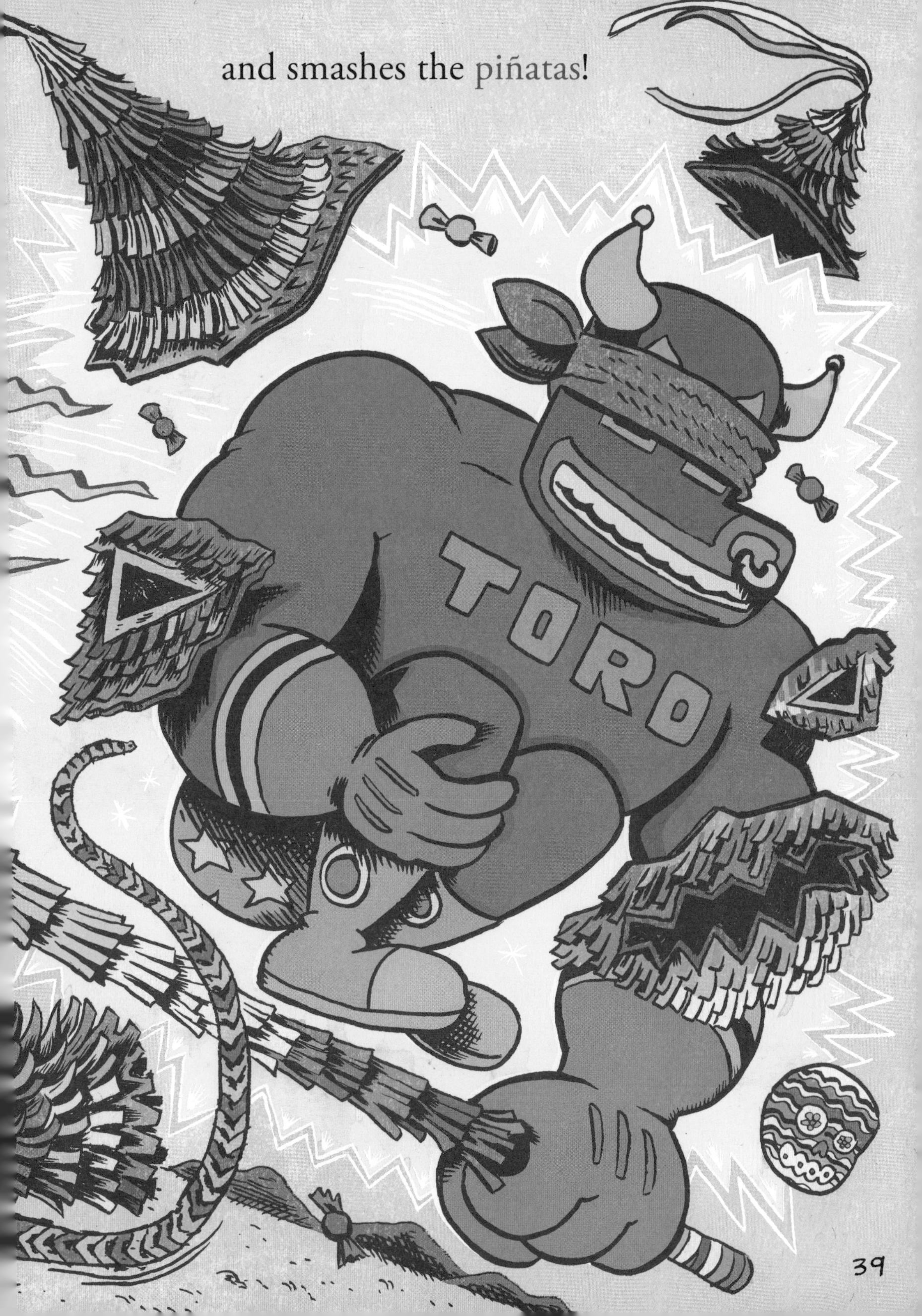
TORO

He crushes the cars

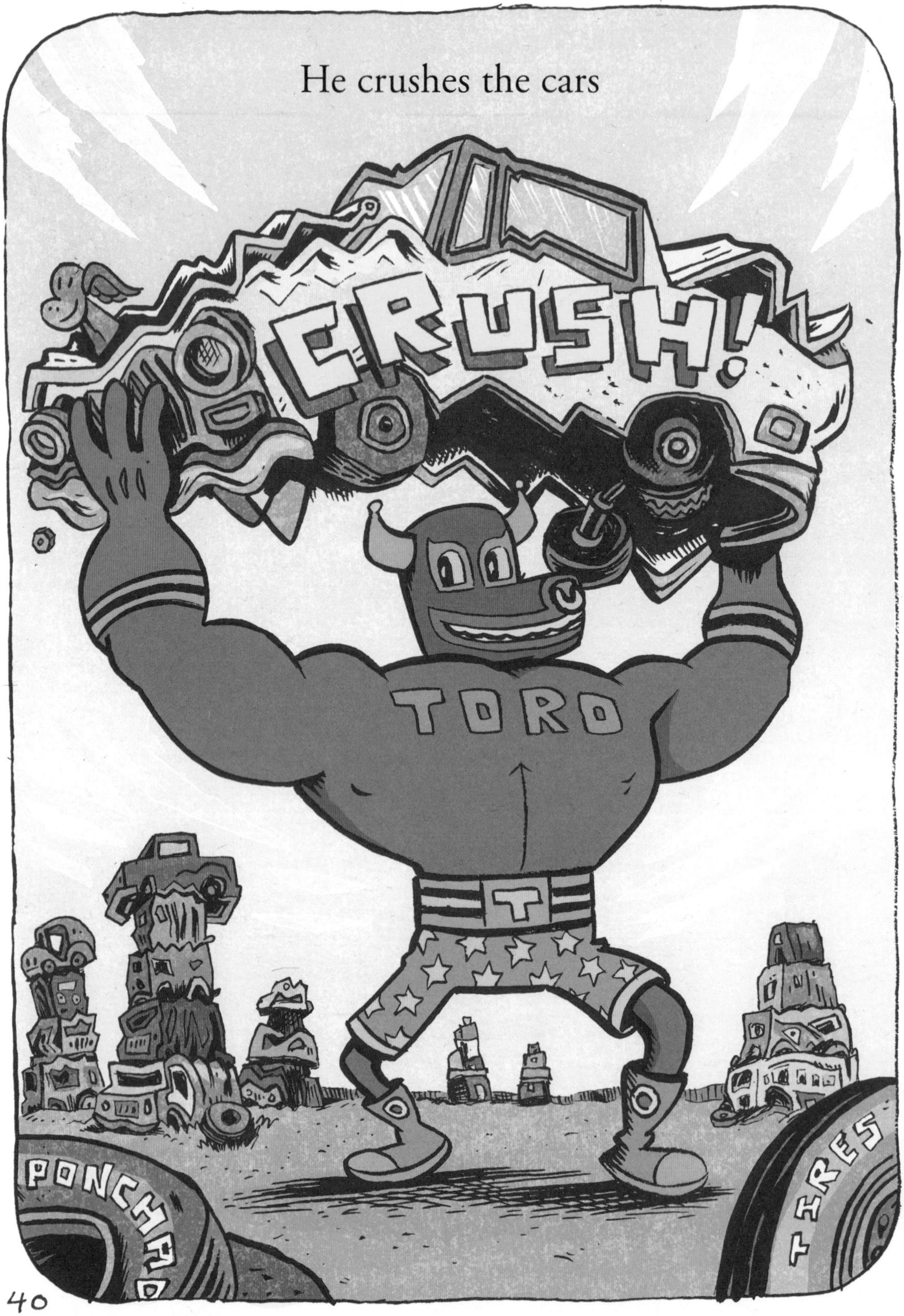
CRUSH!
TORO
T
PONCHO
TIRES

and helps las abuelas cross the street.

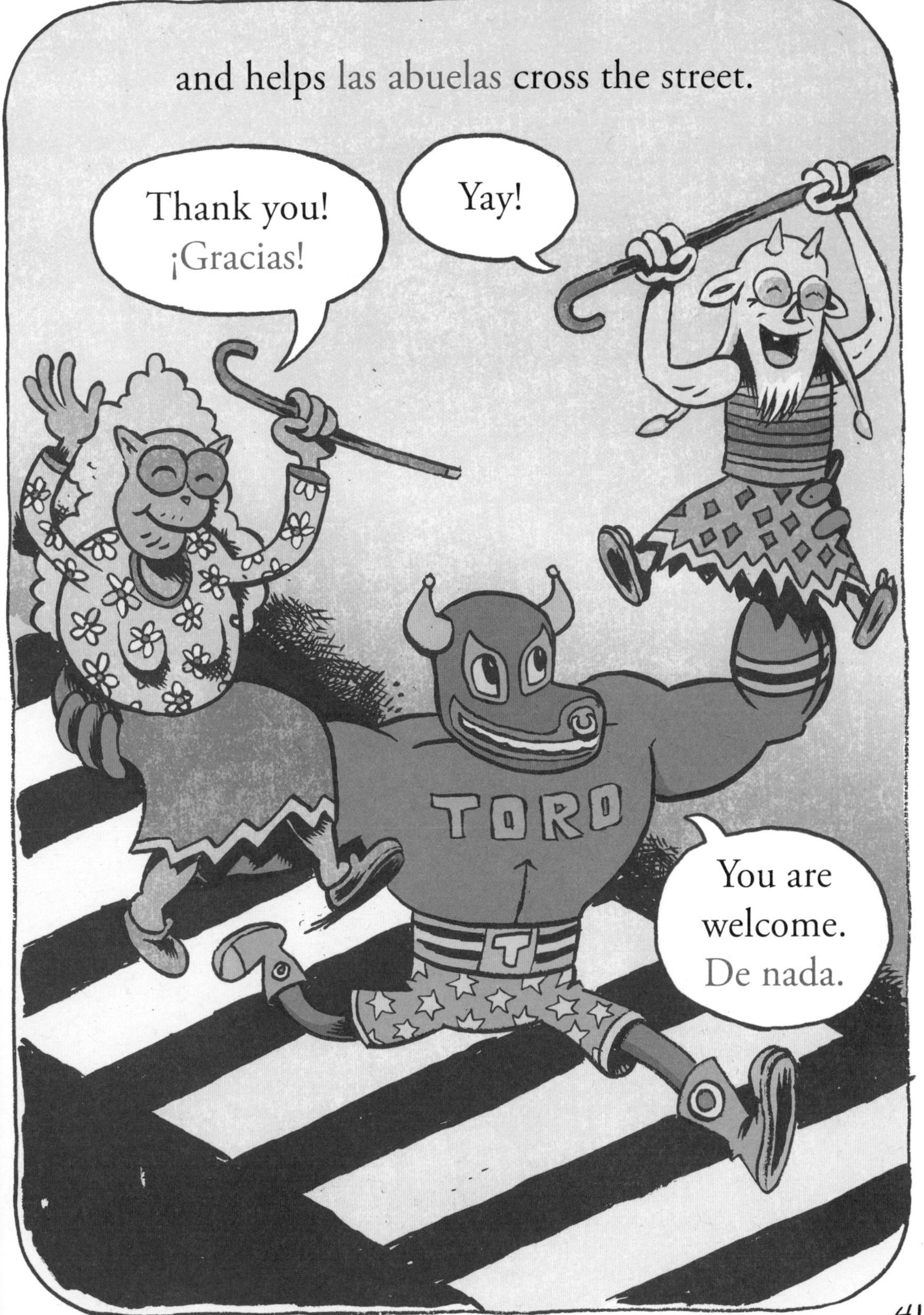
Thank you!
¡Gracias!
Yay!
TORO
T
You are welcome.
De nada.

Day after day, El Toro trains . . .

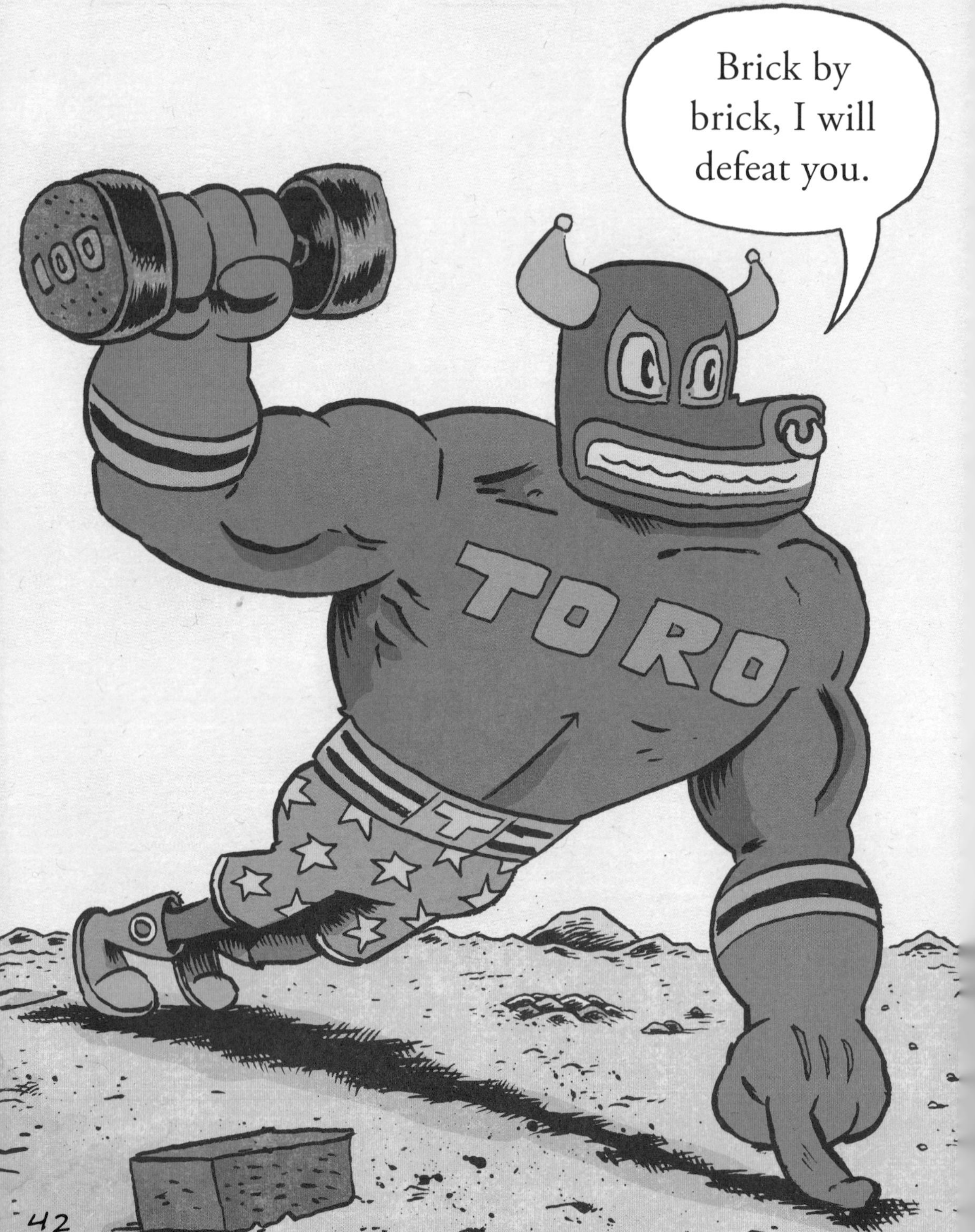
Brick by brick, I will defeat you.
100
TORO
T

El Toro walks toward the wrestling ring.

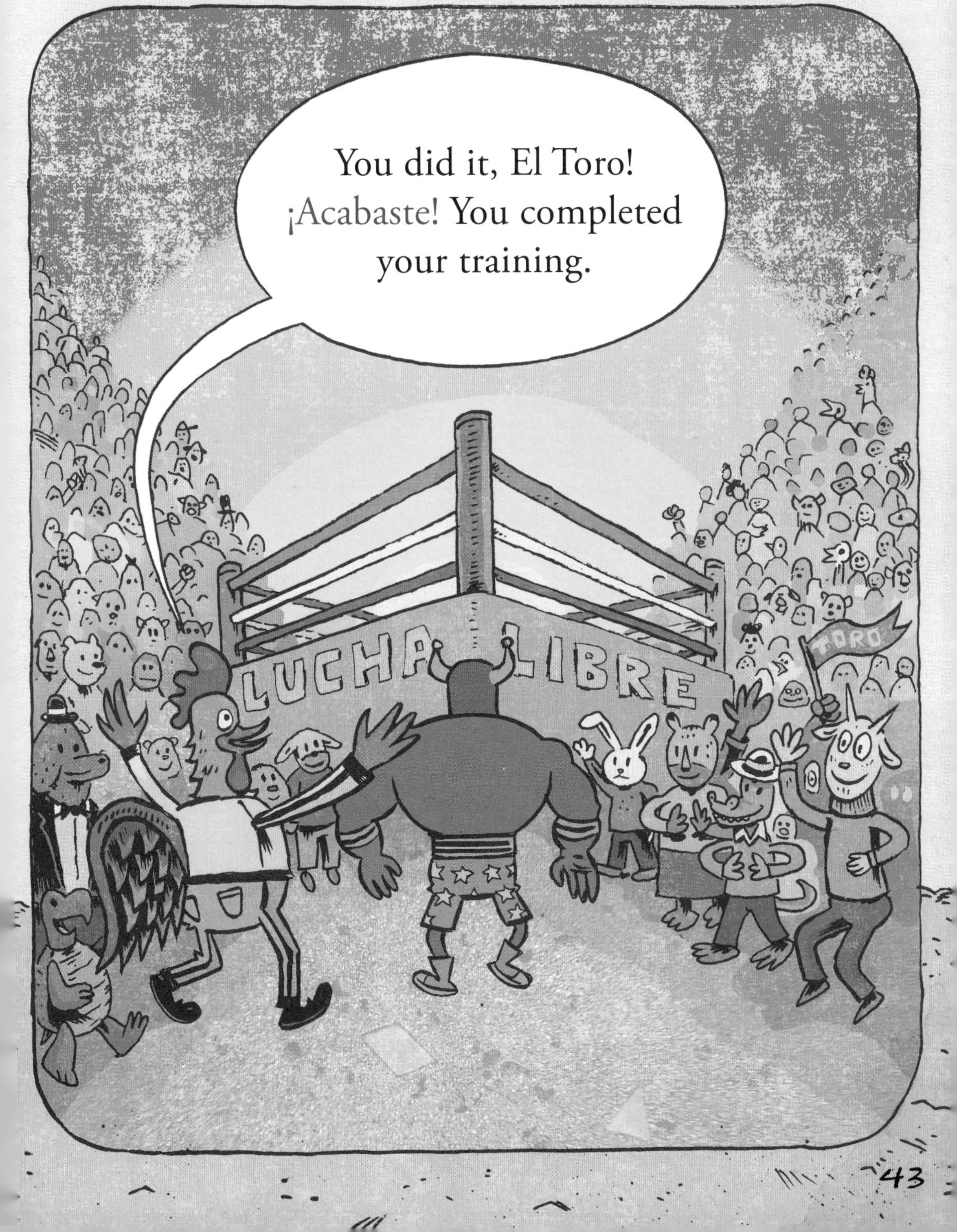
You did it, El Toro! ¡Acabaste! You completed your training.
LUCHA LIBRE
TORO

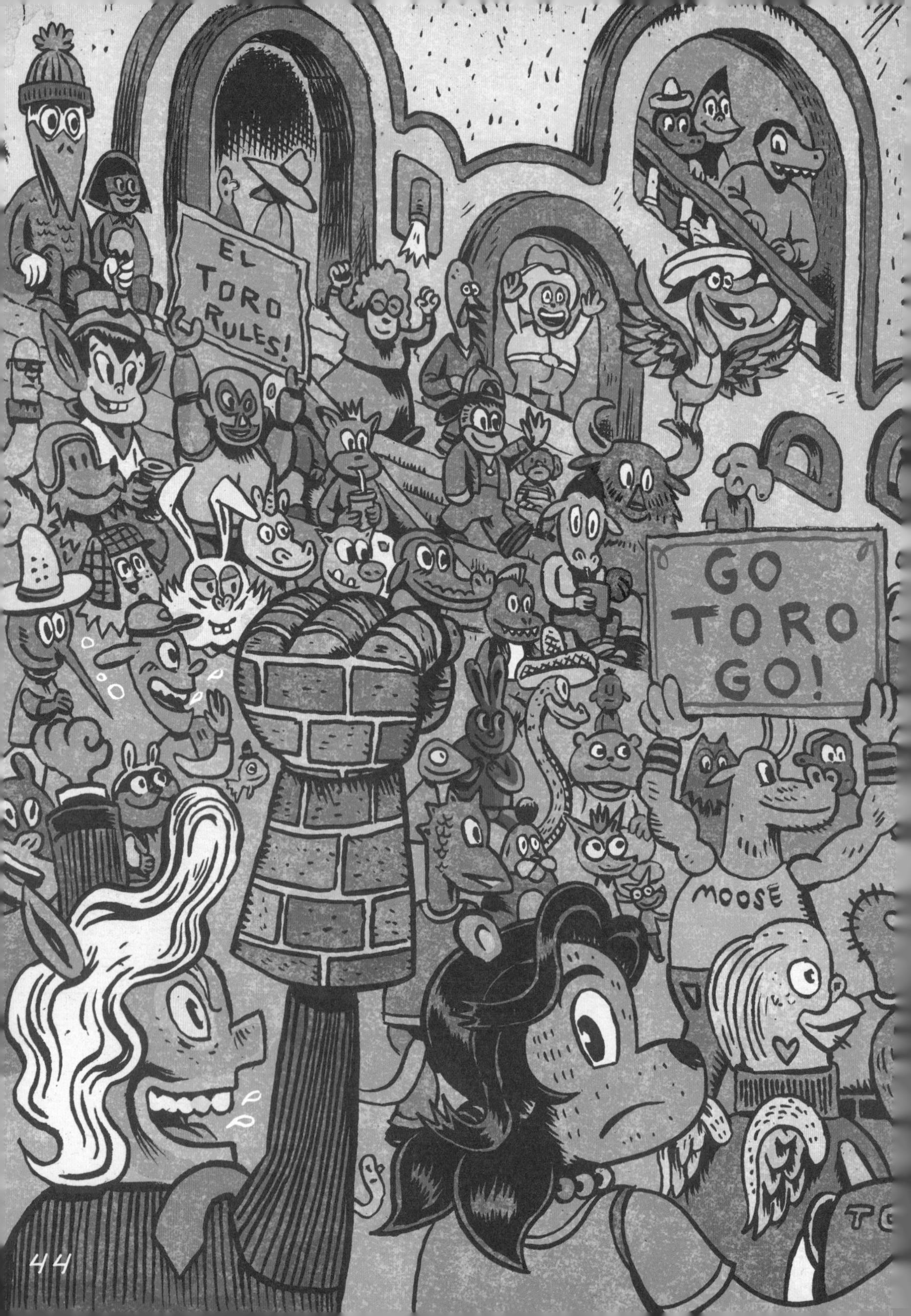
EL TORO RULES!
GO TORO GO!
MOOSE
TO

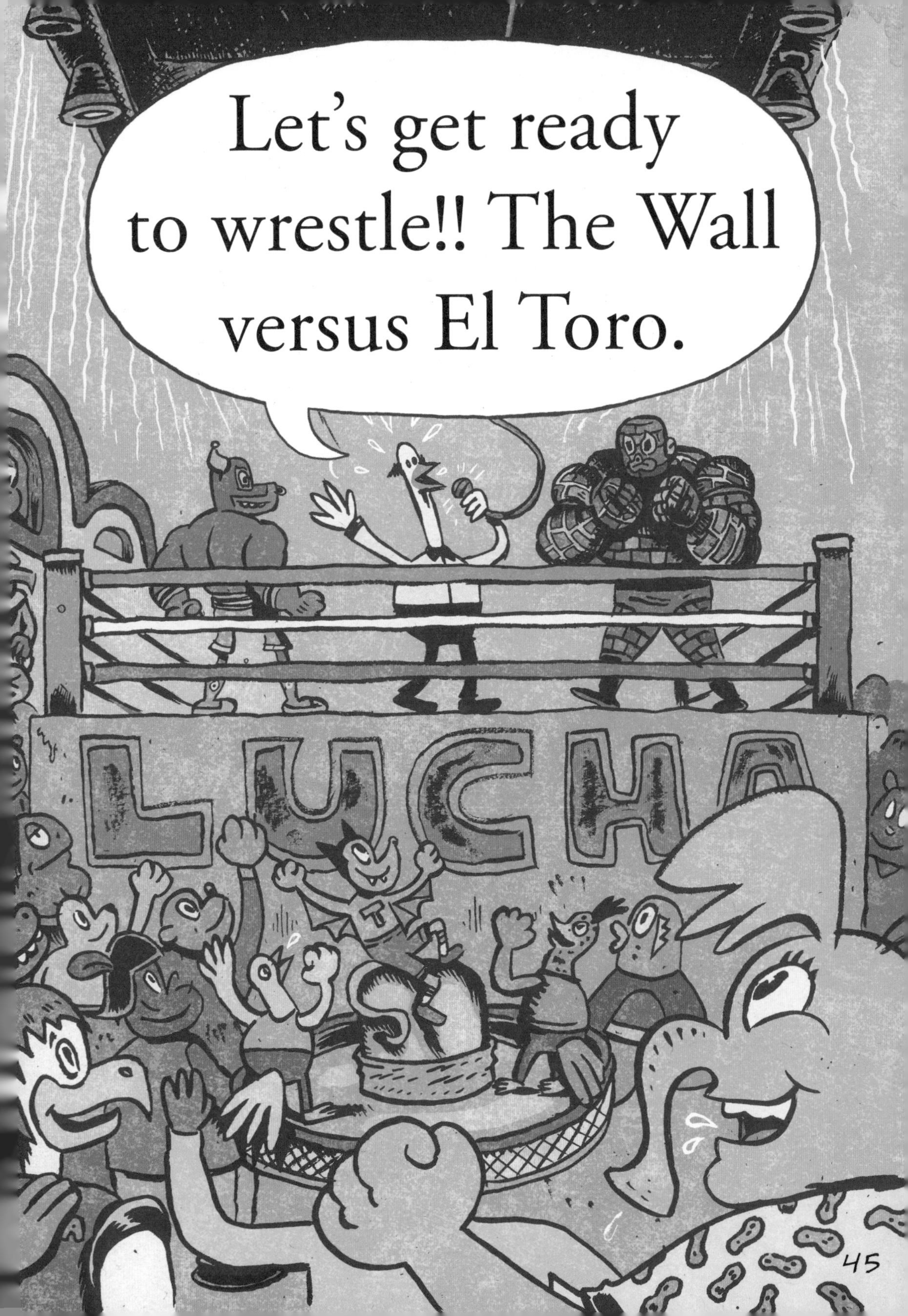
Let's get ready to wrestle!! The Wall versus El Toro.
LUCHA

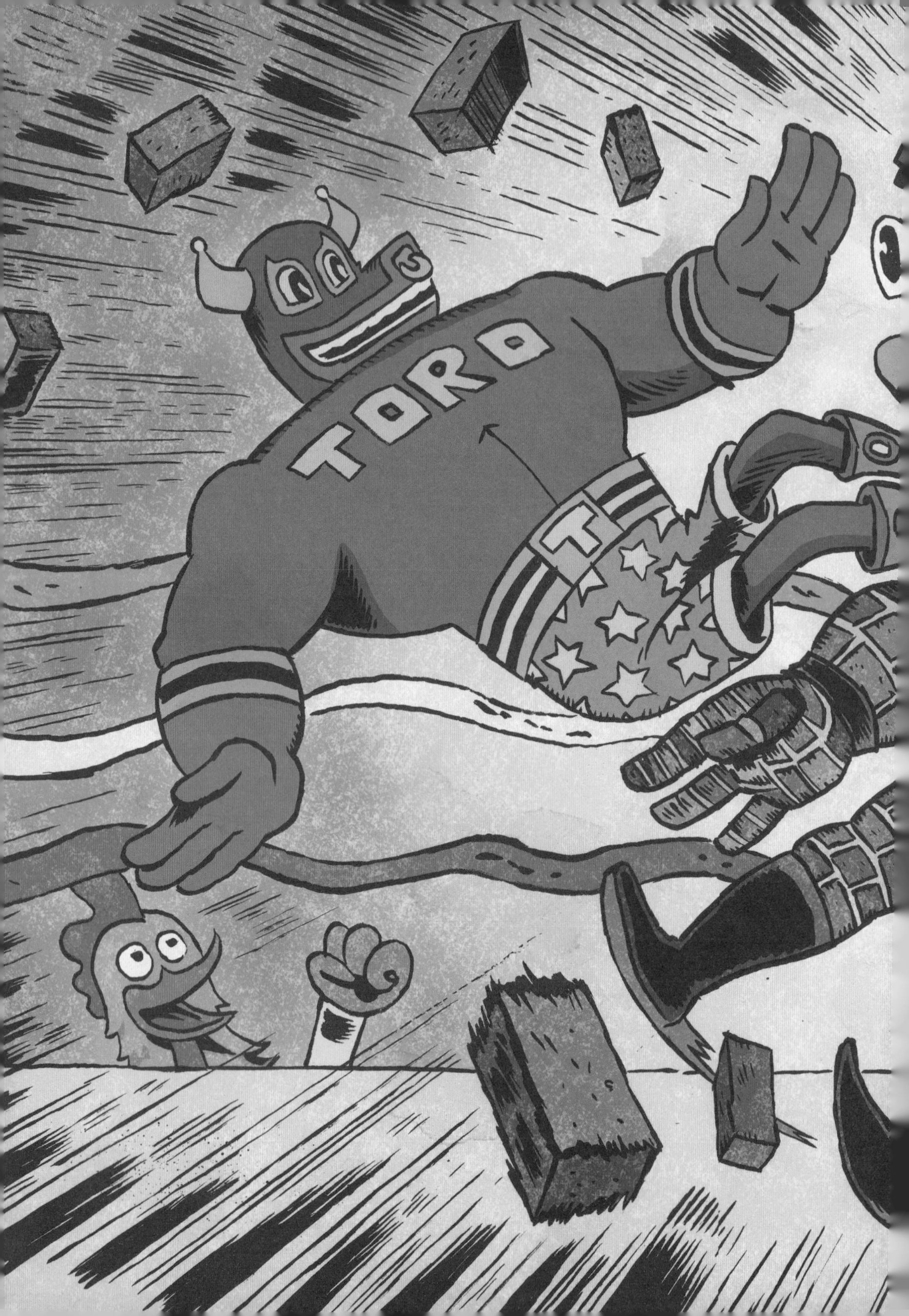
TORO

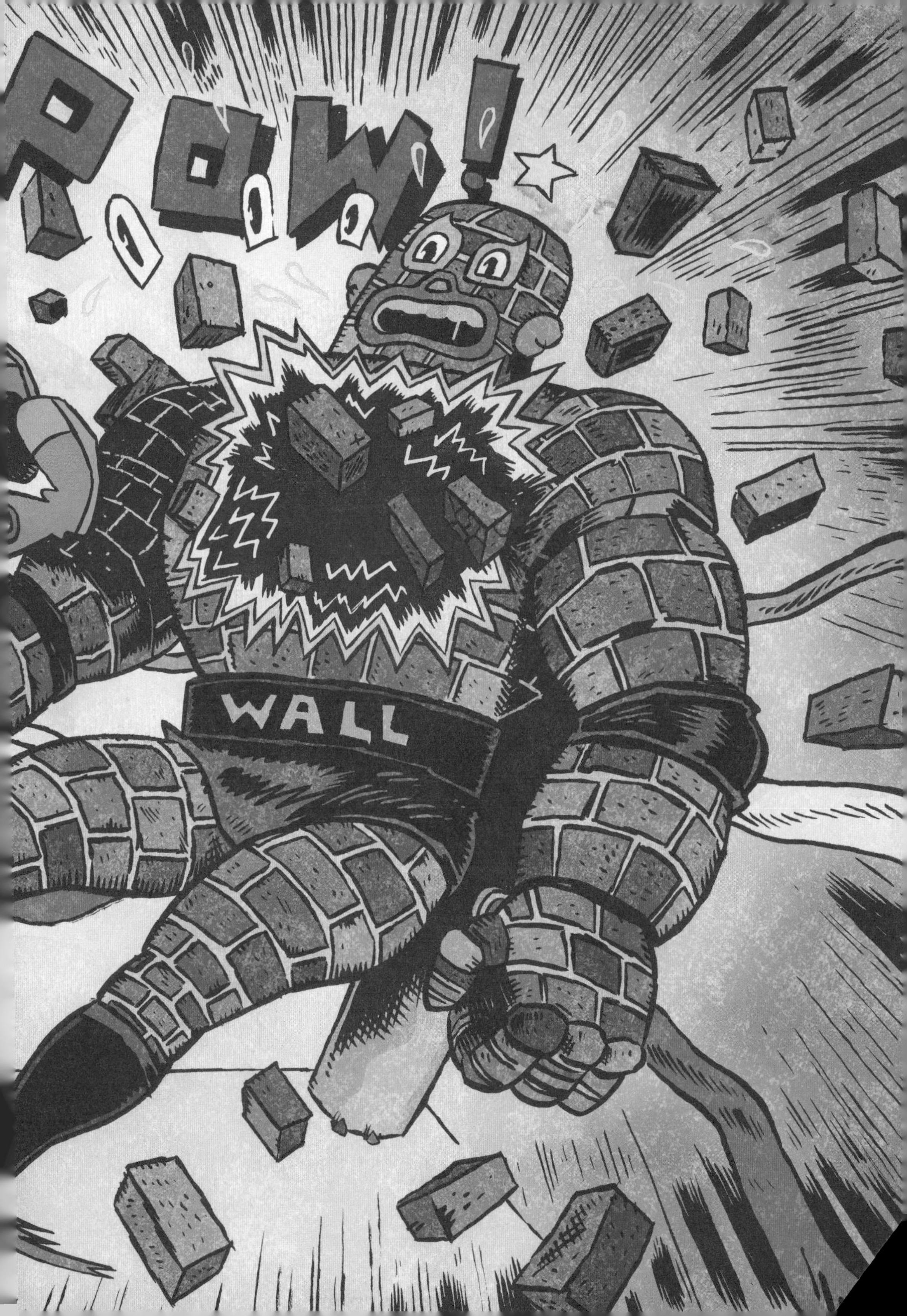
POW!
WALL

To the Mexican boxers I grew up watching with my dad.
They taught me that you need a training regimen to become good
at what you do. —Raúl the Third

To Tang for teaching me how to train all day, everyday —Elaine Bay

All rights reserved. For information about permission to reproduce selections from this book, write to
trade.permissions@hmhco.com or to Permissions, Houghton Mifflin Harcourt Publishing Company,
3 Park Avenue, 19th Floor, New York, New York 10016.

Versify® is an imprint of Houghton Mifflin Harcourt Publishing Company. Versify is a registered trademark of
Houghton Mifflin Harcourt Publishing Company.

hmhbooks.com

The illustrations in this book were done in ink on smooth plate Bristol board with Adobe Photoshop for color.
The text type was set in Adobe Garamond LT Std.
Hand lettering by Raúl Gonzalez III
Design by Natalie Fondriest

The Library of Congress Cataloging-in-Publication data is on file.

ISBN: 978-0-358-38038-2

Manufactured in China
SCP 10 9 8 7 6 5 4 3 2 1
4500816108

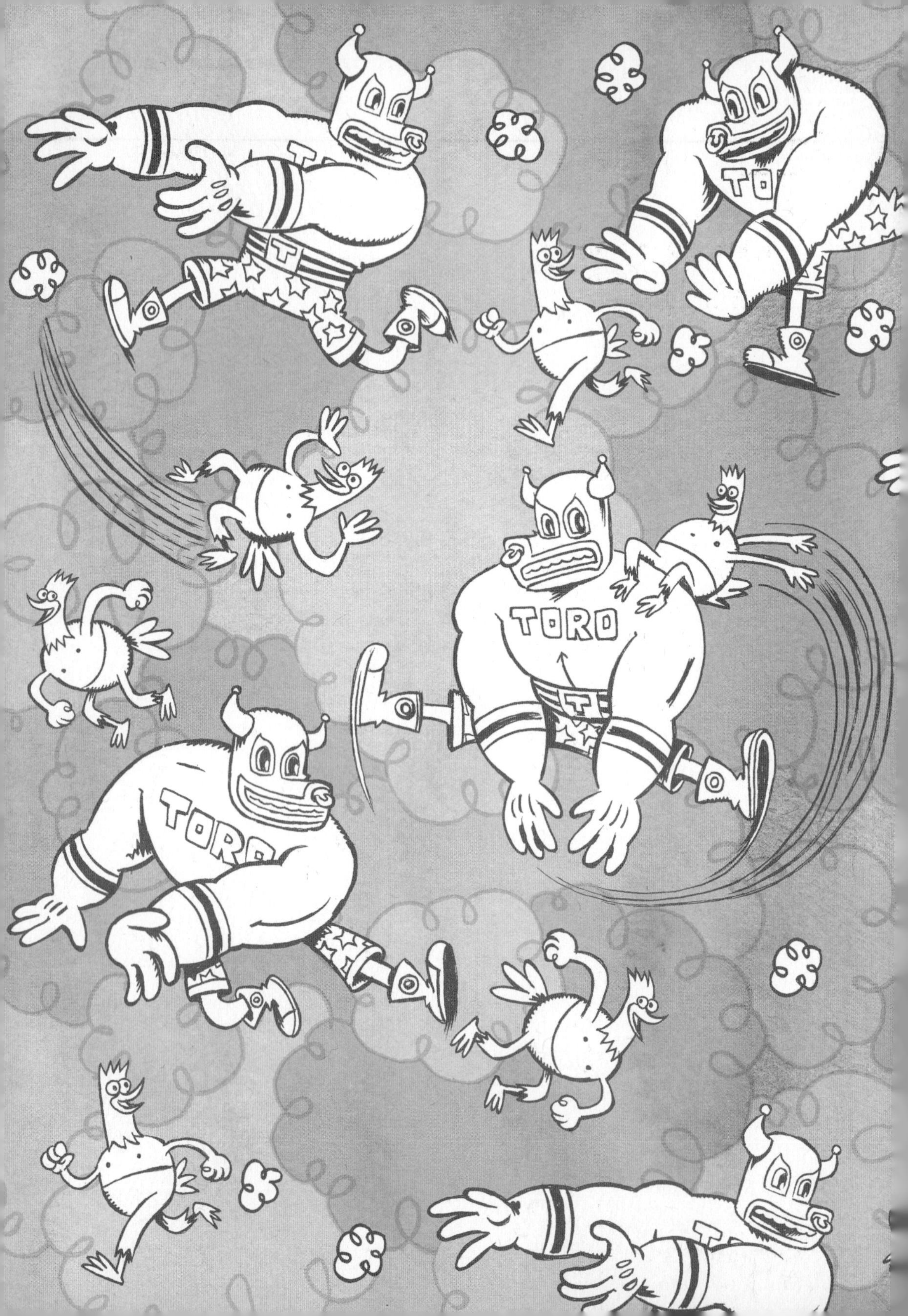
TORO
TORO
TORO